THE BRINK

THE
BRINK

STORIES

AUSTIN BUNN

HARPER  PERENNIAL

NEW YORK • LONDON • TORONTO • SYDNEY • NEW DELHI • AUCKLAND

HARPER ● **PERENNIAL**

THE BRINK. Copyright © 2015 by Austin Bunn. All rights reserved. Printed in the United States of America. No part of this book may be used or reproduced in any manner whatsoever without written permission except in the case of brief quotations embodied in critical articles and reviews. For information, address HarperCollins Publishers, 195 Broadway, New York, NY 10007.

HarperCollins books may be purchased for educational, business, or sales promotional use. For information, please e-mail the Special Markets Department at SPsales@harpercollins.com.

Some of these stories, in slightly different forms, appeared in the following: "How To Win an Unwinnable War" (*The Atlantic*); "Griefer" (*Zoetrope*); "Getting There & Away"(*FiveChapters.com*); "The End of the Age Is Upon Us" (*American Short Fiction*); "Ledge" (*One Story* and *Best American Fantasy*); "Everything, All At Once" (*The Sun* and *The Pushcart Prize Anthology*); "When You Are The Final Girl" (*West Branch*); "Curious Father" (*Bloom*).

Philip Larken's "Aubade" reprinted with the permission of Farrar, Straus & Giroux and Faber and Faber Ltd.

FIRST EDITION

Book design by Sunil Manchikanti

Library of Congress Cataloging-in-Publication Data
. Bunn, Austin.
  [Short stories. Selections]
  The brink : stories / Austin Bunn. -- First edition.
    pages cm
    ISBN 978-0-06-236261-2 (paperback)
      I. Title.
    PS3602.U55A6 2015
  813'.6--dc23   2014029048

ISBN 978-0-06-236261-2

15 16 17 18 19   OV/RRD   10 9 8 7 6 5 4 3 2 1

For my mom,
who dreamed this first.

The mind blanks at the glare. Not in remorse
—The good not done, the love not given, time
Torn off unused—nor wretchedly because
An only life can take so long to climb
Clear of its wrong beginnings, and may never;
But at the total emptiness for ever,
The sure extinction that we travel to
And shall be lost in always. Not to be here,
Not to be anywhere,
And soon; nothing more terrible, nothing more true.

PHILIP LARKIN, "AUBADE"

Contents

THE BRINK

How to Win an Unwinnable War

The catalog comes in a sharp white envelope, "PLEASE FORWARD" written in his father's cursive on the outside. Sam paws the return label, which reads, "Governor's School for the Gifted and Talented." The governor has noticed him.

"Tell me it's free," Mom says. "Free would be nice."

But Sam would do summer school even if he had to drain his savings account or extend his paper route. He likes school—the sweet octane of highlighters, the systems of reward—with a pureheartedness most seventh-grade boys reserve for taking advantage of themselves. He skims the courses, Euclidean Geometry, Beginning Japanese, and stops at a "late addition." How to Win a Nuclear War.

Suddenly, Sam knows exactly how he'll spend the summer.

Tucked in his closet is a "go bag" with Band-Aids, sunblock, shin pads, and the cinnamon granola bars no one wants. As far as he is concerned, nuclear holocaust is the only thing worth thinking about. Back in the winter, when Mom left his father and they moved into the apartment, she promised Sam a gift, a prize for coming. He asked for a plastic barrel to store

fresh water. She bought him a fern instead, a fern now brown-
ing on the front stoop. According to Sam's estimates, Princeton, New Jersey, sits just outside the kill zone of Manhattan.
He has a chance of surviving. He and his mom have a distinct
chance, and the idea that he could save people orients him like
a polestar. The year is 1987.

"Seriously? You want to take that class?" Mom asks, setting
down her book, a hardcover for nursing school. The book fas-
cinates Sam, the photographs of gashes and lesions and people
with cowed, empty looks, as though no matter how pink or
black the wound, no matter how dire, they still might yawn.
"This is your summer we're talking about."

"But summer school doesn't cost anything. It's *zero dollars*," Sam says. He digs around in the box of Fig Newtons
tucked next to her on the chair. One is left. That is their rule
now, living together as a team. Leave one behind.

"Promise me that when you find out how to win," she says,
signing her permission, "you'll tell the governor. Tell everybody. Even if I'm not around."

She will always be around. That is the whole point of winning.

"Now," Mom says, "go get us more cookies."

The first day, Mom drives up the narrow road of the local
college. Workers in white suits rip long strands of ivy from
buildings, and Sam is reminded of that movie, the one about
the war against the plants, the one where we lose but there is
an island.

"Your father will get you after," she says. "Don't let him take you to pizza again. That's too much pizza happening." Then she pulls her lips over her teeth like she has no teeth and, with her pinkie, scrapes a neat edge to her lipstick. The blouse she's wearing, shiny and blue, is made from whatever hot-air balloons are made from. She wants to look pretty for someone, and Sam wants to tell her this is wrong. They need to go backward. They belong back with his father, at the house in the woods, with a basement and kerosene and a well, instead of the duplex apartment in town where, after the bombs, they could be forced to eat people.

She idles the car at the entrance to the hall, a stone building with a sign out front that says, "Gifted This Way." "No grades here, right?" Mom asks.

"Right," Sam says, even though he wishes there were grades, the proof that he matters to an indifferent world. For the past year, he has had a problem with caring too much. A C on an algebra test made him weep. When the art teacher called his mug an "ashtray," he vomited. Later, in his diary, Sam wrote, "MUST DO BETTER," and then practiced his telekinesis on a pencil, marshaling invisible forces in his favor.

Mom brushes his bangs. "And tell your father you need a haircut."

Inside, the conference hall has the carpeted, low-traffic feel of the Unitarian church where Mom now takes him— stacked folding chairs, chandeliers, the sense of things moved to the side to make way for more boring. Kids scatter across the room with books in their laps, pretending to read. Nearby, two redheaded twins fight in slow-motion. One says, crazy-eyed and arms spread wide, "Enter Thunderdome!"

Sam finds a table with lanyards and takes his—his first official designation, and already he feels remarkable. At the front of the room, a bearded professor sits on a stage in hiking shorts and short-sleeved Hawaiian shirt. A giant metal bowl of poker chips rests in his lap. He has the lordly face of the one with the directions, and his fingers comb and coddle the black hair on his chin, like scratching something private and dark.

The professor whistles with two fingers. "We're going to start with a game," he says, and Sam's heart sinks. He is terrible at competition, the neighborhood of failure. The turdlike mound of his mug returns to him.

The professor holds the bowl over his head like an offering. They are going to trade chips. Two blue chips equal one red chip and two green chips equal one blue—Sam only half follows—and in the end, only five chips in their hand will count.

"Count toward what?" asks one of the twins.

The professor says, "You'll see."

A mechanical door sighs open at the side of the room, and a boy in a wheelchair motors inside. Sam notices his white sneakers, splayed out to each side and unscuffed, the way Sam wants but can't have because the world keeps making more dirt. A Panama hat shadows his face. The rest of him looks small and shrunken, like he's been through the dryer. His plaid, long-sleeved shirt is buttoned all the way to the top, but his throat is a tendony stalk and doesn't fill the collar. An older boy follows him in, carrying his backpack like it's a dead animal. "Yowza," he says. "Opening ceremonies in Dorktown?"

The boy in the chair tilts his head up to him. "You may leave, Teddy."

The older kid dropkicks the bag into his lap and gives all of them the finger as he exits. The handicap door wheezes back into place.

"Please excuse my brother," says the boy in the chair. His yellow eyes swim behind heavy glasses. "He was raised by snakes."

The professor asks someone to get a lanyard for him—Ethan is his name—and Sam is nearest. Once more, the professor explains the rules and then dumps the bowl of chips on the carpet. Kids rush forward, giddy and screaming, a vortex of spaz.

As Sam hands Ethan his lanyard, he grabs Sam's arm and pulls him close. His breath is a hot fog, the pallor of his skin almost butter. "Get us the red and blue ones," Ethan says. "As many as you can." A cough rumbles from inside him, and Sam steps away—he doesn't want whatever Ethan has—and dives into the fray.

Since he's started to clean the living room rug with his fingers, Sam has no problem working at carpet level. A girl with braces scratches his hand in desperation, and he scratches back. A boy stumbles and spills his hand, and the others set on the chips like feral dogs. Somehow, the carpet is covered with black chips and white chips, and Sam doesn't remember the professor saying anything about them. Now the black and white chips are all that is left.

At the end, Sam improvises a bowl with his shirt and Ethan plucks five red chips from it. This makes sense for a moment, since Ethan can't reach the floor. But that leaves Sam stuck with the remaining colors.

"Don't you want to trade?" Sam asks. "Aren't we supposed to?"

"No, not really," Ethan says.

The professor whistles again. The game is over. Ethan drives his wheelchair to the front of the room, where the professor counts the chips and Ethan, with the five red chips Sam gathered for him, ends up the winner. "Congratulations, you get to choose your country," the professor says, and Ethan flashes the headlights on his wheelchair, basking in praise. He doesn't even look at Sam, who feels lied to, or at least not told everything other people know. Like two weeks ago when Mom dropped him off at the video arcade with a twenty-dollar bill, and he came home with most of it unspent, feeling thrifty and proud, only to find the front door locked and a strange jeep parked out front. He knocked until she answered in the silky gown she only wore at night and her hair all crazy, and she said, like she was sad to see him, "Oh, Sam, please, help me out here."

Sam needs lessons in people.

At the afternoon pickup, his father asks, "Who blew up who?" Kids stream out of the hall into the waiting cars. Sam slumps into the passenger seat of his father's truck and watches as an elevator hoists Ethan into a van driven by his mother.

His father feeds in a Beach Boys tape in a preemptive bid for affection. It's the one tape Sam said he liked. On the dash sits a twisted up bag of peanut M&Ms, opened already and therefore tainted, the ransom for spending another weekend with his father.

"Okay then," his dad says to the silence. "What do you want for dinner?"

"Pizza."

On his old bed, in the house in the woods, Sam pours over the class textbook, a catalog of ballistic missiles—their ranges, payloads, blast perimeters. He reads about the Centaur, a missile that scissors the clouds and guides itself by the stars. It's more powerful, more beautiful, that way: a missile that looks up. Now he has a favorite missile. He wonders what the stars will see the day the war begins, the whole planet brightening, then going gray like a dead bulb.

Sam cinches a piece of floss around his two front teeth, to close the gap between them. He wants to teach them to get in line, and the dull ache in his gums is the proof that they are learning. The sounds of the television rise up through the floor. Downstairs, in the dark, his father watches sports with the unsalted, least-fun peanuts. The house is dim and cavernous now, since they left. Mom was the one who kept on the lights, and his father would follow behind, turning them off.

Earlier, in the garage, his father showed off the car engine he had taken apart, the grimy pieces laid out on newspaper like bones from a dig. The front grille of the VW van, the one his father uses for his house-painting company, gaped in front of them, a face with a staggered aspect. His father pointed out the ways the pieces came together, the Wite-Out dashes he'd made to remind him how they joined.

Sam thought: my father will be useful in the afterscape.

He sets the book down and stares out his bedroom window. The night is clear and the trees behind the house almost purple. A plywood plank covers the old well, now just a ring of crumbled stones. Sam can make out, nestled up in the crook of the maple tree, the tree house his father built for him. If necessary, Sam can raise the rope ladder and survive up there. His fingers trace the fire emergency decal on the windowpane, the one they passed out in school. "KID INSIDE," it says. No one will notice this sticker in the war, Sam thinks. No one will be looking for stickers.

"Sambo," his father says at the door, beer in hand. "What's happening?"

Sam tells him about the arcing paths of Centaurs and Tridents, twenty times more powerful than Hiroshima.

"Jesus Christ," his father says. "That's what they're *teaching* you?"

"That's the homework."

The next morning, his father comes with him to class. Having your parents, the Big Robots, come with you is a sign of weakness. Sam separates himself as much as possible, trying to look like he barely recognizes the man who tinfoiled the leftover pizza for lunch and who quizzed him on the state capitals on the drive.

Ethan motors over. He's dressed in the same shirt and pants from yesterday, only different colors. His Panama hat dangles from one of the handles of his chair.

"Is that your father?" he asks.

"Maybe," Sam says. He watches his father shake hands with the professor and point Sam out. The professor's beard is bigger than his father's, and Sam theorizes that he has unknown capacities, subterranean holds of grown-up.

His father waves him over, and Sam drags himself to the professor's side. "If anything we do in class makes you feel uncomfortable, you can opt out, right?" he says.

This close, Sam notices a gap between the professor's front teeth, just like his own, and he feels a sudden, covert allegiance.

"I'm fine," Sam says.

"Good," his father says. "As long as it's on the up and up." He holds out his palm. "High-five."

But if Sam high-fives, in front of the class, the gesture will cost him. Enjoying the company of your parents is a form of offsides. His father pats him on his shoulder instead, swipes his bangs out of his eyes. "Be good," he says. "And tell your mom you need a haircut."

The class unfolds a world map, the size and wrinkled texture of Twister. Last class, they chose their countries. As the winner, Ethan took the U.S.A., large country/large resources, and became the most hated person in the room. Out of spite and boredom, Sam chose an island, a speck in the Pacific. Guam.

"You can't sit this one out," the professor said to him. "Look at the Falklands. Look at Cuba."

"I'm looking at Cuba," Sam said. "Now what?"

"Little places have a way of changing history." This is the professor's way of making Sam feel better, except stories like this only make him sick to his stomach. He doesn't want to change history, just outlive it.

The professor circles the room, handing out army men and single matchsticks to represent missiles. "First we'll see who survives," the professor says. "Then we'll find out *how* to survive."

Ethan gets a whole matchbox and an entire freezer bag of army men. The map fills up with their allotments. Sam takes his single army man, a grenade thrower, and bends the arm around so it picks its butt. He hears the whirr of Ethan's approach.

"Take these," Ethan says. He hands over several army men and a single matchstick. Sam can see the underside of Ethan's chin, where a razor has been. He's old enough to shave.

"What for?" Sam says.

Ethan blinks. "Because you're mine. Guam is pretty much America. Look it up."

Over lunch, Sam befriends the Pacific Rim: Jerusha from Weehawken and Irwin, the Asian kid from West Orange. They eat at a picnic bench outside the hall, under an old oak. The branches are so low that wooden support beams prop them up and the twins kick at them, trying to dislodge them, anything to do damage. Irwin puts his retainer on a leaf. Jerusha's parents wanted her to be at Christian camp, she says, but she thought she'd be "more useful" here. She tells Sam that the leftover pizza he's eating is two percent rat droppings and that she saw an angel over her house once.

"How did you know it was an angel and not an alien?" Sam asks.

Jerusha looks stricken. "Because he smiled."

Irwin pounds the picnic table. "That is not proof of anything!"

At the entrance of the hall, Sam sees the professor crouch next to Ethan. A tube now runs over Ethan's ears and up into his nose, like an old person in a hospital show. A tank props up in the netting at the back of his chair, and Sam tries, telekinetically, to turn the knob on the tank and cut off whatever gas Ethan needs to survive. But it doesn't work. The opposite happens: the professor brings Ethan over.

"Space for one more?" the professor asks, and they make room reluctantly. Ethan lays out his lunch in his lap: a baloney sandwich and chips. Sam can hear little puffs of air jetting up Ethan's nose.

"Do you have AIDS?" Irwin asks.

Ethan sighs. He does not have AIDS, he says wearily. His lungs don't work right. He's on a list, and if his name comes up, they're going to cut him in half and give him new ones.

"Cut in half, like side to side or top to bottom?" Sam asks, and Ethan places finger at the notch at the base of his throat. "From here," he says, drawing his finger down his shirt to his stomach, "to here."

"Lungs from a dead person?" Irwin asks. "*Awesome.*"

Ethan turns to Sam and kicks him gently. "When we get back, I want you to attack Russia."

This is just what Sam was afraid of, that he'd become another small thing in a game played between people. He just wants to be ignored, the way he spent the entire basketball season—on the bench, whispering multiplication tables, praying for armpit hair. Sam balls his tinfoil into a hard nut. "What do I get if I do what you say?"

Ethan says, "You get to die for a reason."

On the last morning of the world, light breaks over the ocean and Sam is there, on the beach, in Guam. The people of this island nation make necklaces from shells or eat donuts, whatever they do. But the beach is all his. Sam's father and mother lounge on the big towels, talking like they haven't talked in a long time, like they want to keep talking. Sam pokes at a dead sand crab, a weird piece of armor the ocean threw up. He is tucked between his parents, feeling gathered and protected, when he sees the white contrail of a Centaur streak up, a fast and terrible rip in the sky . . .

Sam holds a matchstick in his fingers.

His missile, the one from Ethan. His turn.

"Somebody's going to win this war," the professor says, pacing behind them. "Who is it going to be? Is it going to be you?"

Across the map, Ethan nods at Sam privately, the way a gangster in a movie cues an execution. Sam has no strategy. He's afraid that Ethan, up in his throne, has unspeakable

powers, the gift of knowing that you're only alive because
somebody else died. But with the matchstick in his grip, his
Centaur, Sam sees his life from above. Suddenly the map, the
game, doesn't matter. Sam can be Guam, the speck in the Pacific, the small thing passed between people.

Or he can be the missile.

He arcs the match over the ocean, toward America. He
aims for Ethan, for home. When it lands, Ethan whispers,
"What are you doing?" and Irwin makes the blowing-up noise,
a rumble with puffed cheeks. The professor says, "First strike.
Guam against U.S.A. Interesting . . ." Soon, every missile on
the map will launch, the planet turned to stone, the lesson lost.
But Sam is, already, elsewhere.

That night, Mom's new friend Latrice reclines on the couch,
smoking languidly and turning Sam's photo cube over in her
hand. It's all vistas of his father: grilling, up a ladder, holding
Sam at birth when he was still jaundiced and Chinese-looking.
Sam recognizes Latrice from the Unitarian church, from the
part of the service when people stand up and speak. Latrice
talked about women's rights and black people rights and
coming together for a better tomorrow and Mom clutched
Sam's hand. Latrice is the only black person there, so it's like
she is all black people.

"Your father looks like a nice fellow," Latrice says, and sets
down the cube. She pulls her denim jacket tight. Her hair
intimidates Sam, so solid and dense, like the black foam at
the tip of a microphone. On the right pocket of her jacket

is a button: the radioactive symbol and the *Ghostbusters* line through it.

"My dad's really strong," Sam says. "He loves to hunt." Sam sits in the rocking chair, making it rock as much and as irritatingly as possible. His bangs curtain into his eyes, and his mouth is half-full of the chocolate bar she bribed him with.

"Do you see him much?"

"All the time," Sam says. "He comes here too sometimes, just to watch the house. See who is coming and going. My mom doesn't know."

This time, Sam's lie is bold, riskier. Latrice raises her eyebrows and turns toward the window. The blinds are up, the drapes wide, and the streetlights make the parked cars look only half-there. Latrice's jeep is parked at the curb, the sticker for the Princeton Seminary in the back window. By her worry, Sam can feel a trajectory taking shape, the flickers of a future impact.

"Oh, and thanks for the candy," Sam says. "My dad doesn't let me eat sweets."

Latrice checks her watch.

"Candy and smoking," Sam says. "He really hates both of those things."

Latrice stubs out the cigarette. "Your dad sounds like a piece of work."

Mom descends the stairs in her feathery blue blouse except now it's too tight because Sam put it in the dryer, trying to be helpful. She smiles weakly. "The babysitter's still not here?"

Sam shrugs. The babysitter is not coming. She called, but Sam took the message and forgot to tell.

"I can make us something," Mom says. "I have some left-over chicken."

Latrice exhales and her breath just keeps going. "I'm vegetarian, remember?"

Sam sticks out his tongue with the plop of chocolate. Mom fingers a cigarette from Latrice's pack. "Not what I need right now."

Every class, they war, and every class, the earth dies. Over two thousand nuclear warheads exist, the professor tells them. But only *twenty* detonations are necessary to erase all life, and they have a hundred matchsticks. The twins, playing Russia and Brazil, can't keep from bullying the planet. Ethan, with his arsenal, makes a point to tick off Guam in every strike. Sam just waits for the nuclear winter to snow all civilization. Once, the class gangs up on the twins and rains its stockpiles onto Russia all at once. But even then, even with their entire population killed, Russian missiles retaliate automatically. "It's called The Dead Hand," explains the professor. "Even when they lose, they win."

Jerusha begins to cry. "I hate this game," she says. "All it is is getting killed."

The professor taps his fingers together. "Very good, so what are we learning?"

Jerusha's sobs fill the quiet room. At least she believes in angels, Sam thinks. At least she has someone to get her when the time comes.

"Anyone?" the professor asks.

Ethan says, brightly, "New game."

His father's voice booms from underneath the house-painting van. Only his boots stick out.

"How's your mother?"

Sam leans on the van's bench seat, unbolted from the car and propped against the garage wall, listening to the radio. A newscaster says that a West German plane landed in Red Square, that this might be the beginning of something. Sam spins a gasket around his fingers. A gasket is the ring of metal that goes between other metal, his dad said, to make them join. These lessons usually bother Sam. He doesn't want to learn what his father wants to teach. But now, here is this bright fact of gasket. Even words can grow up and make themselves useful.

Sam stares at the hanging lamp over the car, puzzling an answer. His father doesn't know about Latrice, who has been sleeping over and leaving paperbacks on the coffee table and storing sand she calls "fiber" on the breakfast shelf. This morning, when his mom was in the shower, he saw Latrice naked, lying in his mother's bed, scratching the pale bottom of her foot. Her nipples looked like light switches. If he told his father all of this, his father would go quiet and far away.

"She asks about you," Sam says.

The cranking and banging stop. The newscaster says the pilot was a boy.

"She does? What do you say?"

"I told her," Sam begins, "that you have a new friend. And her name is Jerusha."

His father glides out on his sled, turns down the radio. "Why did you tell her that?"

The lies are getting hard for him to think through. First strike is easy. But second and third and fourth go further than he can see.

"I wanted her to know you have somebody."

"I have somebody," his father says. "I have you."

This is his father trying to make him feel worthy. But Sam knows that he's the consolation prize, what you win when you've actually lost. "It's not the same."

His father taps a wrench against his leg. "Your mother just needs some time. Just wait."

But how much time, Sam thinks. Because there won't always be time. Japanese people got hit so hard by light they became permanent shadows—an old man with a cane, a mother with baby stroller—and their shadows won't even wash off the ground. Time ends. He's seen the pictures.

From here on out, the professor says, class is about the after. "Let's say we hear the big alarms. Let's just say we have five minutes before a ten-megaton explosion over New York City."

Sam's eyes go instinctively to the row of high windows in the room. It is noon and clear, but the weather doesn't tell you anything—it was beautiful that morning in Hiroshima too. In his mind, he can see the cloud trace of arcing missiles like rows of close-rule paper in the sky.

"Imagine nobody is coming for us," the professor says. "Now what?"

Their suggestions go up on a blackboard. Store water from the water fountain. Cover the windows. Ration their lunches. Sam has walked through these steps in his head so many times they are polished smooth with worry.

"I want to be with my parents," Jerusha says. "In heaven."

The professor tugs at his beard. "I'm okay with that."

Jerusha lies flat and stares up at the ceiling.

"What are you doing?" Irwin asks.

"I'm waiting for the angel."

The professor picks up a coffee can with a plastic wrapper over the top. "Does anyone know what this is?" Sam has seen the designs in *Protect and Survive*, the booklet he ordered from the Department of Defense. "It's a fallout meter," Sam says. "It measures the atmosphere. It tells you when you can go outside."

"Very good," the professor says, and for the rest of class they make their own meters. The professor passes out the empty cans, and Sam notices flakes of instant coffee stuck to the bottom. A dank and spicy smells rises out. They pour in the crushed gypsum, which looks like white dirt, and hang two squares of aluminum foil above it on kite string.

"How do we know these things work?" Ethan asks. His fallout meter looks broken, the string sagging. He has gypsum powder sprinkled on his pants.

"Well, we won't know," the professor says, "until it happens, really."

"But then we'll be dead."

The professor points at him. "And that is a distinct possibility."

"That's retarded," Ethan says. He motors over to the trash can and dunks his fallout meter.

"I'm okay with that," the professor says.

Then Ethan rams his chair into the door to the outside. But it doesn't open and he's stuck there, his chair straining. He leans over and shoves the bar to drive forward, but when the door opens, his chair lodges in the gap. From the effort, Ethan begins to cough wetly, buckling over and hacking into his lap. It sounds like he's drowning on the inside.

Sam goes to him. Everybody should be able to open a door.

Ethan sits up, his eyes gluey and cheeks flush.

"Fuck off," Ethan says, weakly, and wheels himself outside.

The professor follows Ethan out. He's gone for a long time, long enough for the twins to practice strangling each other until they can withstand wiggling fingers at their necks. Ethan's Panama hat lies crumpled on the floor, and Sam takes it. Through the window, he can see Ethan at the curb, waiting in the sun.

"Ethan is fine," the professor says when he returns. "He had a tantrum like this last time."

"Last time?" Sam asks. "He's been in this class before?" So that is how Ethan knew about the chips and the rules, about the consequences for winning early.

The professor stares out at Ethan. "He'll come back."

Except Ethan doesn't. They finish with the fallout meters

and nobody learns anything except that gypsum tastes like ash and they can flick balls of tinfoil across the room if they do it right. And still Ethan waits in the sun. Nobody comes. Just like the professor said. Nobody will come for them and one day this class, this room, might be all they have.

The next day, Ethan doesn't show. Or the day after. He's in the hospital, Jerusha says. Her parents are friends with his mother, and she said he got to the top of the list for his operation. She brought a get-well card for everyone to sign. It goes around the room, and when Sam gets it, he sees just a bunch of fancy signatures. The card was a chance to practice their penmanship.

Sam writes, "I have your hat."

They never see Ethan again.

On the last day of class, out on the front porch, Mom hugs Latrice and moans softly into her shoulder. Sam is disgusted. His mother never hugged his father on the way out. Latrice doesn't deserve what his father didn't get. He tells Latrice, telepathically, that her time in their lives is coming to an end. As they embrace, Latrice turns her mother slightly so she can scan the street, see who is seeing them.

"I'm going to be late for class," Sam says.

They separate into their cars, but when Mom turns the key, Sam hears just a small click, softer maybe that what he expected. The engine doesn't start. Latrice leans into the window.

"What do you think?" Mom asks.

"No idea," Latrice says. "I won't even pretend." The way she says it, she pretends sometimes.

Sam says again that he's going to be late.

"Latrice can take both of us in her car," Mom says. But that will change the order of things, Sam thinks, the way the future has to happen.

"I can?" Latrice says, and Sam replies, "I don't want to go with her."

Mom massages her temples. "Come on, guys. Work with me."

Latrice studies Sam skeptically, as though she can see through to his secret. But at this point, Sam doesn't actually need to do more than make his loyalties plain.

His mom whispers, "*Shit*."

"I wish you wouldn't swear," Latrice says.

Mom looks up at Latrice with exhaustion. "Really?"

Sam opens the glove compartment, where the covert pack of cigarettes is, and hands them over. Mom snatches the pack from him. "You're not supposed to know about these. Don't know about these."

"We should call Dad," Sam says.

Latrice now seems impatient. She says she has somewhere to be. She has decided this problem is not her problem.

"I'll call you," Latrice says, backing off.

She leaves and Mom goes to the front stoop to sit, fiddling with the fern, yanking off the dead parts. It has more dead parts than green parts. The plant supposed to be *his*, his reward for letting his father go, but it's nobody's plant, put where nobody's looking. He remembers his mom bringing it home, so springy with life, saying, "You need to learn how to keep things alive," but it smelled like crotch, and Sam felt betrayed. The person who could give him a plant as a gift was someone who didn't know him at all.

"Call your father," Mom says. "Tell him to get his ass over here."

Sam is kneeling on the couch and watching from inside, through the blinds, when his father's van pulls up a half hour later. He's come straight from a job, overalls crusted with paint and flecks of white on his cheek and in his beard. His parents face each other coolly, Mom on the stairs, Dad on the lawn with his hands on his hips, as though they don't need a single thing from each other. His mother points to the car, hood up, and his father peers into the engine.

His father does nothing, just looks up at Sam's bedroom window and scratches under his cap. A kind of joy warms inside Sam. This is what he wanted.

"Come here, Judy," his father says.

"No lessons, please," Mom says.

"Just. Come. I want to show you something."

She goes to him. If she would only keep going to him. They stand together at the open hood and consider the damage. Sam knows he's been discovered. His father leans on the bumper. Mom puts her hands to her lips in a sort of prayer, even though the Unitarians only bow their heads.

"Sam, get out here!" she calls through the screen door.

When Sam gets on the porch, his father sees him and says, "Jesus Christ."

"Sweetie, what did you do?" Mom says.

A breeze seems to gather the heat of the day and press it toward him. An old woman in a robe walks by with a little dog and stares.

"I cut my hair," Sam says. With the kitchen scissors. All by himself, while they waited for his father.

Mom sits on the top step and pats next to her. Sam joins her, his go bag between his legs. She runs her fingers through his hair and asks if he knows that they love him. But it's a stupid question. Loving someone is easy—look at Latrice! And *knowing* someone loves you is useless, like knowing the name of a bird.

"You broke the car, didn't you?" she says. "And you told some fibs."

"Fibs?" his father says. "That's the word we're using?"

Mom gives him her look. "Do you know what he said? He said you come around at night and watch me."

His father sighs and scratches at the flecks of paint, scraping them off.

"Why?" Mom asks. "Why did you do it, Sam?"

Under his breath, his father whispers, "We know why."

"If you don't tell us, sweetheart . . ." Mom says, and he can see her hunt for terms. "We'll have to take you out of that class."

"We need to go back and live with Dad," Sam says.

Mom takes his hand and brings it to her chest, like it's

broken and you make it better by holding. "If you want to go live with your father, you can do that, Sambo," she says. "You can. But I can't."

His father turns away, and his chest begins to convulse. Seeing his father cry is like watching a building collapse when someone you know is inside. It is raw and close and terrifying. Sam shudders too, and the tremor grows inside, a tremor that started months ago with his mom waking him up, late at night, in the house in the woods, to take his hand and whisper, "I need you to be brave, sweetie, because tomorrow we leave."

A row of black cars have parked outside the hall, golden seals on their doors and flags on their radio antennae. In the shade of the oak, a group of men in suits and sunglasses wilt in the heat, their suit jackets hung on the branches. They seem to be waiting for Sam, a gang of fathers ready to administer punishment.

His father parks the car at the hall entrance. He's wearing sunglasses to hide his eyes. The Beach Boys tape flips over, another harmony starts. His father looks straight through the dash. "As smart as you are," his father says, "one day you're going to grow up and forgive us."

"How do you know?" Sam says, stepping out of the car. "Nobody knows anything." Growing up is pure luck. Two thousand warheads are ready in their silos, waiting to grow up. If the class taught him anything it's that every place in the world is inside the kill zone. He grabs his bag, with the Band-

Aids and the granola bars and water bottles, all of it rolling around in a big swill.

"I'll wait for you outside," his father says. "I'm not going anywhere."

So Sam will need to find a distraction, a way of sneaking out. Because he's not going home, not going back. He's on his own now, as he always was and will be. The moment he steps inside the foyer, Sam hears clapping. The main hall is crowded with parents and other professors, strangers he hasn't seen before, the whole summer school, and he can't make his way in. Spread across the carpet, students sit attentively, preparing for a transmission. On the stage, a fat man in a blue suit jingles the change in his pockets. He surveys the room with a smile like he's at the top of a mountain and they are the trees. The room is hot already, sun glaring through the windows.

New Jersey believes you will do great things, the man says to the crowd. New Jersey is, frankly, astonished. "Would any of you like to ask the governor a question?" the professor says, at the edge of the stage.

One of the twins raises his hand. "The Russians have these missiles so that if all their cities burn up, these missiles fire automatically and everybody dies," he says. "Can we have that?"

The governor dips his head. "Excuse me?"

"It's called The Dead Hand," the twin says.

"Very good," the professor says.

The governor glares at the professor. "Good lord, what's this all about?"

He shrugs. "This is what they've been learning all

summer," he says. "This is the state of our world, the one you have made."

"You must be kidding."

Jerusha raises her hand and asks, "Where is your special cave when the war starts?"

The governor stammers. "When the war starts . . . ?"

An emergency blare shatters the air. Sam takes his hand off the fire alarm. At first, no one is sure what's happening or where to be. Then a mother screams, and frantic parents crush into the room, toward their children. The governor presses toward the exit. He wants out, to his special cave, but he'll never make it. He is caught in their panic. "Stay inside!" the professor yells to the room, but the children are fine. The children look calmly up to the windows, ready for incoming.

Griefer

Our favorite world was almost over. Tonight, when I dropped, a countdown clock hung in the game sky. You couldn't miss the bright yellow numbers up in the twilight. There were just days left in the Also, to be who we were. I zoomed to the old homestead in Gjajan, where I built my manse and gardens and dug my private sea, where Aremi came to me, but the place looked like it was having a stroke—just a throb of pixels, a cloud of bad data that fluxed and ate at the terrain. Years of questing wiped away, and I could take nothing with me, like a refugee from a dream. I moved closer, to brush the metaphysics of it all, and my machine seized. The Core was as stable as a stilt on a stilt.

I dropped again, this time to the foothills of Origin Park to wait for Aremi. We had agreed to find each other here, the last place they'd wipe. The Park debuted on the first compile—ganked from topos of the Acropolis—and the texturing was smeary and low-res, not like a place but the memory of a place you drove by in a car. The engineers kept it around as an artifact, proof of how far they'd come. I zoomed to the edge of the gray-green butte. Below me, the city stretched out on five peninsulas into the ocean, a hand on a mirror. Hundreds of players hived at one of the city terminals. The Also's com-

poser, this nineteen-year-old kid who made the game sound
like a nail salon, was having a live farewell jam. If I boosted my
speakers, I could just perceive the twee.

At the horizon, the dull gray wall of the Exit sparkled with
tiny match flares, the lights of hundreds of players stepping
through. For the last month, the Exit had been moving closer,
absorbing grid. The engineers designed it so that players could
off under their own power, ceremoniously and unalone. Tran-
siting through the Exit was the official way to de-install. Since
the game worked its way into every cranny of motherboard, if
you didn't off through the Exit you'd have bits of the game clut-
tering your OS, trying to recompile. We'd all go through it soon
enough. Above me, players streaked by on aerial, hunting their
home populations. The processor couldn't handle the air traffic, couldn't render all the individual skins, so they went naked,
like fuselages, arcing in an empty sky. The sight depressed me.
Another humiliation in a windless world. That's how it would
be when the lights went out: we'd all be looking for someone.

I ping'd Aremi, who would understand, who still needed to
tell me which world was next so I could follow. But she wasn't
on yet.

/yo get over here. It was Rrango. His userpic popped up in
the dash: a koala with an eye patch, smoking a cigar. He was
off in Saturnalia, helming an end party for our raid group.

/i need your fat ass for confession tennis, he ping'd.

/hang tight. waiting for someone.

Rrango was my spawn brother, born the same instant on the
entrance platform and trapped there until we figured out how

to loft. (Notoriously, the Also had no instructions. Part of the appeal, the high barrier to entry.) He worked in Silicon Valley for a start-up launching its own alt-world, and he was always trying to mess with the game parameters. Changing species on every quest. Maphacking for grid he didn't have the points to see. For a while, he had a crew of Chinese digging a pit mine for Alsonax, so he could build this player mod—part amusement park, part nightmare—he called Bewilderville. But then the start-up tanked and his paycheck evaporated, so we had that in common.

These days, Rrango citizened 24/7. He knew about the Cessation Event before anyone. Apparently, the Also had been bought by a Chinese company that ran its own massive alt-world and they couldn't get two systems to integrate. Ours, the lesser, was turning off. Silicon Valley thought alts were gashes anyway, Rrango said, money pits of freeloaders, and since he worked out there, I trusted him. For all I knew, the Chinese didn't even exist.

/Aremi? Rrango ping'd. *Dude: she is a BOT. Don't get played by a program.*

That was Rrango's theory, one of many.

/r i g h t, I answered.

A figure zoomed me. A female, but not Aremi. Blue troll hair spun off her head like some giant curl of frosting. Her chest swelled out grotesquely—one of the cheaper, trashier player mods dialed up to the max—and when she landed, her skin layered on: a rune-keeper robe with flared cuffs. Now I recognized her: Melanak, the first woman I sync'd in the Also. I hadn't seen her for months.

/trying to boink your way out of here? I ping'd.

/hahahahaa, sweetie. just one last costume change.

Red sores began to appear on her face, and white tendrils worked their way out from inside. They looked like the hairs on a coconut, quivering with weird life. I'd heard about the pox—a viral experiment the engineers had released to get players to de-game early—but had yet to see it up close. I will admit she did not look sync-able.

/kiss me? she ping'd.

/think i just puked on the inside. is it contagious?

/nope. pox is soulbound, she answered. */tied to your play hours.*

So the engineers were punishing us for our loyalty, and Melanak was the loyalest. What I knew, or what she'd told me and what I agreed to believe, was that Melanak was a forty-year-old EMT from Tampa, a beta tester for the Also. I'd met her by chance on one of my early quests when I had the bad idea to unzip a Kraken all over his lair. She was knobbing on intersect mode in the Gjajan market when I asked for help, and she enlisted long after she'd leveled past. Some people prefer to give rather than receive. With the Kraken, Melanak became my meat shield, taking damage and guiding me through the attack step by step, like the older woman I'd always wanted and never had.

/sent u something, she ping'd. */parting gift.*

A photo flashed in my dash. I already had several of Melanak's pics—at first, they were tame, like a family shot she'd taken at Sears with her boyfriend and teenage son. Then came a run of sexy ones I hadn't asked for. She had hauntingly massive areolas and the stoic face of a Ren-faire butter churner, and though she wasn't exactly hot she was always game. There was affection there, between her and my hand and a few pumps of Jergens in the home office. When I opened the newest photo, it took me a minute to recognize his face. It was Melanak's son, grinning back, holding a black cat upside down, its paws lashed together and head hanging lax, the way a cat never does. You could tell by the cockeyed angle it was a selfie, camera at arm's length.

/*wtf?* I ping'd.

/*what do u think*

/ . . . *cat is mucho unhappy.*

/*what do u think of me?*

/*? you? your son?*

/*hahahahaha.*

My breath stalled. /*who is this?*

/*;p*

I pushed away from the machine and made sharp angles with the crap on my desk. In the other room, my wife Jocelyn chopped a salad for dinner and hummed the NPR theme, and the sound of real life brought me back into myself. Melanak had been a woman when I first met her—I knew that, or wanted it with the full force of my personality. The ruse was too long, her syncing too dexterous and knowledgeable for a teen to fake. We'd game-chatted all the time, her voice Southern and bossy. Four hundred pounds maybe, but female. Except, the engineers had let the protocols slip, and the voice-chat function stopped working weeks ago.

/tell me when, I ping'd.

/when what faggot?

/when you hacked mommy's account.

/maybealways lol

I lunged at him with a Reverse Time Knife, but Melanak had levels on me. He lofted, out of reach, and spun in a circle, the blue coif perfectly still. The engineers had never figured out the breeze physics and never would.

/where's mommy?

/dead. got her head in my lap.

/sicko, I ping'd. *good luck with 8th grade.*

/good luck with being a faggot.

I blocked him, silenced his pings, and Melanak zoomed off anyway, taking his disease with him. From the twilight, white pixels started to drift down. There had never been any seasons in the Also. You always dropped into luminous summer. But as I waited, it started, at last, to snow.

"So . . . did you get out at all today?" Jocelyn said as she dropped her bag at the front door and collected the spray of mail at her feet. "I'm guessing not."

The lemon scent of Endust hung in the living room—I misted minutes before she got home, to give the impression that I'd spanked up the place. The ghost velocity of the Also persisted inside me, the feeling of roller-skating long after you've stopped roller-skating.

Jocelyn scanned the bills, and my eyes ached from the hours staring at the screen, where objects didn't reflect but gave light. I willed myself to see her, to take her in. Her charcoal pants and blue blouse looked assembled from a drop-down menu—her cloak of professionalism, she called it once.

"I took a walk," I said. Actually, that had been yesterday. I sometimes harbored details to deploy them. "The locksmith has a help wanted sign in the window."

"You're thinking . . . keys?"

From my back pocket, I removed the paper with his phone number.

"You only wrote that down to show me, though, right?"

"Maybe. But don't I get some points?"

She untucked her blouse, and I recognized her more.

"You do, Josh. You get a million points."

Jocelyn darted up to the bedroom and returned barefoot, in a T-shirt for a band neither of us had listened to since college. We started on our dinner, a mound of salad greens, and she asked about the business school applications she'd printed for me. Yes, I saw them. Yes, they were in the office, stamped with coffee rings. School was her dream, not mine. We ate on the couch watching the television—the comedy news from the day before—almost laughing but not quite.

"Listen," she said. "I just know something amazing is going to happen for you. And it's not keys."

Something amazing like a phone call from Renfield in city planning, inviting me back to work. She registered the purple glow from the study, the twilight of the Also on my monitor, and sighed.

"How long is it going to be," Jocelyn said with disdain, "until that is finished?"

A cold breeze swept through me. An enormous grave had been dug, but the dead were in a distant country Jocelyn had never been to and didn't care about.

"Days, I guess," I said.

"Good," she said, and took her salad bowl to the counter. "Because I want you back."

She grabbed her bag and went up to the bedroom. The door shut, and I felt abandoned. At first, years ago, Jocelyn had pretended interest in the game. Then she tolerated it, and we kept a running silence going, like it was some nerd dialysis I had to do but that nobody—not our friends, not her mother— wanted to hear about in detail. But then in March, Renfield called me into his office and asked me about the huge traffic on the network pegged to my desktop. I told him I was getting stronger, just not the version of me he could see. He raised his eyebrows and said, "We've had a good run," and I disap- peared into the Also for a weekend, questing a Dissolution Cube. That Sunday afternoon, one task short, Jocelyn yanked the power strip. She said she was living with a teenager, which sucked, which needed to change or we were over. The cords hung in her hand like the bouquet of dead snakes I ended up with after draining the Moat of U'mkatam. So we posted a cal- endar in the kitchen where I recorded my hours. Now, when she came home, she'd palm the CPU to see if it was hot.

Through the blinds, I watched the sunset fire through the windows of the unfinished condos across the street. The developer had gone bankrupt during the construction, and a gate surrounded the ground level. Stacks of Sheetrock and buckets lay abandoned on the cement floors. A blue tarp flapped from a wood beam, tugged by the wind. I lingered on the couch, heartsick for the next thing in my life, for some future that could bear weight, while I listened for a ping from the office. The sound of company.

Aremi.

I met her two weeks ago, when she was forty minutes old. I had encircled the homestead with a perimeter alarm, and she tripped it. When I found her, she was just a nub of black hair sticking out of the render. Somehow, she'd lofted from Entrance Rock and backhoed herself in deep. As we neared the end, you could find pockets of null all over the place.

/this interface blows! she ping'd, her head thrashing in the busted polygons.

Eventually, Aremi maneuvered free. She'd outfitted herself in classic moon elf, green skin with red eyes and flared ears. It was first choice on the pull down. Her hair fell in two braids down to her chest, disappearing into a maroon cowl. Pretty much everybody dumped the Mordor crap long ago for bespoke player designs like BabyMomma, DimeBag, IceQueen. I skinned in EmoPrince, mostly for the syncs.

I pulled up her player profile. She'd sketched it—only diehards fleshed them out—but she said she was in grad school in Arizona, mostly "taking baths" and "avoiding my adviser."

/what's your field? I ping'd.

/how'd you know?
/your profile, you wrote it
/doh! psych.
/here for research? on gamers?
/on loneliness.
/srsly? I ping'd. */I should leave you alone then.*

It was an n00b mistake to ask too many questions too fast. And I didn't want to creep her. So I backed off, let her drive herself, and answered her pings when she asked. We lofted over the hedge maze that I had planted out the back of the manse. I've always had a thing for labyrinths, the original alt-worlds, and Rrango used to invite crowds over to lose themselves and sync in the bushes or whatever. It'd taken me a year to earn the Alsonax to buy the grid and build it. The bright-green walls sprang two stories tall, so once you were in, you were in. Along the paths flowed a series of connecting pools, bordered by statuary of all the creatures I'd pwned—from world bosses down to lair dogs. At the exit, where all the water sluiced to, lay my sea.

/you designed all this? Aremi asked.
/pathetic, eh?
/no, impressive. i mean i had no idea . . .

And for the first time in months, since I stopped working and Jocelyn looked at me as though I had another few mistakes in me, I added up. A stranger saying that I had not wasted my time. This is what the Also does: it feeds you people.

/all this will be wiped soon, I ping'd. */you know the Also is ending right?*

/endings better than beginnings, she answered. */last song beautifuler than first.*

And I thought of Jocelyn with her novels, and how she always read the final sentence before starting them.

/so who are you? she ping'd.

/32 yr, 5ft11. 235lbs (losing ;))

/ew. don't care. I meant: why help me?

/like being a tour guide.

/don't you have friends? or no friends in the game, just players?

I had this small, warming hope that she might become the one thing from the game I could take with me.

/have friends. but new friends better than old friends. interestinger.

/so not a word!

/what about: don't want to be alone when the lights go out.

Aremi went aerial and dusted me. I chased her, and for the rest of the night we did this thing where I'd zoom her and she'd fling herself away. Everybody goes through it, the I-can-fly moment. It's half the appeal of the Also, but eventually, she flung herself away and signed off. No good-bye. A minute later came a ping, slowed by traffic through the Core:

/alone at the end? but we will be.

I spent an hour idling in Origin Park before Aremi finally showed. She was quieter than normal, slow to ping, as though she had come only for my benefit.

/RL aggro, she said, then: */correct usage?*

I needed to wow her.

/there's so much world left to see, I ping'd. /how about a tour?

/show me!

We tethered together and flew through my quest history, every place we could re-achieve—the Lair of the Kraken, the smoking Manhatta ruins, the dungeons of UnderAlso. But viewed on aerial, buried in the new snow, the sites looked small and unpersuasive. The Lair of the Kraken without a Kraken deboning players is a pretty much a cave with clip art. We'd achieve one vista, Aremi would ping, /next, and we'd go. I tried to impress upon her what had been undertaken. In an empty Moon Faire, we downed sinister mead and let our screens blur. We launched together in a catapult, thrown out over the sea. At the giant bones of Dnarak the World-Eater, I told her how thousands of citizens had brought it down. It was the best night in-game I've ever had, a civilization rising up, the hail of weapons like a punishing cloud.

/this why you play? she ping'd. /so you can war? so you can win?

/here more vivid than every place else i know.

/new question: how has the game affected home life?

/i'm research now?

/you were always.

I didn't care. Her attention was an extra sun.

/new question, I ping'd. /how many others in your research project?

/so far just you. feel special?

/feel lucky.

/my question now.

/ok: game makes me feel less lonely. but there are different kinds of lonely.

/how many?

/11.

/what # is this?

/#6. lonely with 50% chance of not-lonely.

/you married? she ping'd.

I went to the kitchen and topped off an OJ and club soda. I'd lied before, of course—about my age, my weight, my actually having a job. It was easier to lie, closer to play than the truth. What answer did she want? What would keep her here, with me?

"Josh, come to bed!" Jocelyn called down from upstairs. "All those old *Twilight Zone*s are on. Even the one about the glasses!"

I hesitated. Upstairs, Jocelyn would be under the comforter, cross-legged, tea set on the nightstand, on the special bamboo coasters. I could see every last detail.

"One sec!" I called back.

/yes, I typed.

/right answer.

/huh?

/am married too, she pulsed. */but might be over. lonely #10?*

My opening, there, flashing. I told her I had to go—it was late where I was—but there was one last thing for her to see.

/the windowpanes, I ping'd.

/?

/the opposite of lonely.

Then I ran upstairs to my wife.

The wooden arch at the entrance of Bewilderville towered above us, strung with purple banners and torches on permanent flame. In these final days, Rrango's pride and glory looked desolate, */like Six Flags after an accident*, Aremi ping'd. */after a maiming!* I ping'd back. An empty rollercoaster whipped along an enormous, vaulting frame, which creaked and strained in the quiet. Rrango was so good he'd cribbed the rumble down to the squeaky nails in the timber. Would anything else in his life ever know such care? On the vacant midway, the World's Fair globe rotated on a programmed loop. Aremi and I zoomed past ghost-face barkers—NonPlayerCharacters triggered by our entrance, luring us to their whatnot—and skirted to the far end, where two squares glistened with ruby light. The Windowpanes. Rrango's trophy, his pièce de awesome. As we got closer, they pulsed and throbbed, aware of us.

/step in, I ping'd.

/explain. don't like surprises.

I told her that when you entered the Windowpanes, you released all permissions on your machine. Every firewall collapsed, and you had total access to your partner's hard drive. Complete transparency.

/too weird, Aremi ping'd. */this whole place is, but.*

Rebuffed, I gave her silence.

/show me yours? she ping'd. */if you want.*

There was no better way for her to know me. The years of music, my pathetic résumé, even the porn folder: the desktop was my life on a tray. */be gentle*, I ping'd; and as soon as I stepped into the Windowpanes, a shaft of red light swept my screen and my keyboard froze. I could feel Aremi enter me, her curiosity whispering through. My cursor moved under her hand.

The figure landed behind her: a saber-tooth in a green tux and combat boots. At first, I thought it was another of Rrango's NPCs on a boo mission. He loved his scares. But then white threads of the pox monstered out of the face like streamers. Melanak could jump skins but not the disease. He strode toward Aremi, his double-jointed legs looking like they were going forward and backward at the same time. The Windowpanes fixed me: I couldn't warn Aremi. My entire system lay open. He could push anything in, to either of us.

/this should be fun! Melanak ping'd.

I jerked the power cord from the CPU, and it went black. My blood thrummed, and I shuddered, back in my body. I'd left Aremi to him. God knows what he'd take from her, or give to her. But I was helpless. Redropping from a crash would require minutes, long enough for Melanak to grief up a shit-ton.

The sounds of the house returned—the television in the bedroom, the central air cycling up, a bird pinging for another bird. Jocelyn creaked open the door. "Josh, why are you on the floor?"

How could she understand? I'd met some colored light that transfixed me.

I told her I felt ill, and she made me lie on the couch. With each step I took I lunged away from myself. She pressed her cool hand to my forehead, checking for fever but also holding me down.

"I have to get back," I said.

"No, you don't." Her face became the face of everyone who knew better. "Look, I understand there are people in that fucking game that mean something to you," she said. "Even people you love. Whatever. Whatever you do with your Jergens. But you have to find a way to say good-bye to it. Because otherwise I'm done."

I told her I needed a walk, to clear my head. Anything so she'd let me go. Maybe I'd check if the locksmith was still looking for someone. Or have coffee in a café, a quiet room with strangers, one of whom could be Aremi and I'd never know. Or visit the library, with the public machines.

I couldn't find her. Aremi's last drop had been hours before, but there was no record of her exit. Her mail pocket was full, and I felt a surge of possessiveness knowing that others had friended her.

Then the library janitors ushered me out.

When I got home, Jocelyn was already asleep on the far end of the bed, facing the wall. As quietly as I could, I put my clothing in the hamper and brushed my teeth. In the mirror, I saw myself, my unemployment beard flecked with white. I looked like a man who'd given up on mirrors. I slipped in next to Jocelyn and left an inch between us. That was the rule when we argued. And I wondered how Aremi slept—on her side, with her husband behind her, like this, with space enough to feel alone? On the nightstand, Jocelyn's laptop hummed in sleep mode, the light from it a tiny moon toggling on and off.

On the final day, I dropped into a blizzard. Flakes drifted in the foreground no matter where I turned, like in the movies, the weather tight around the characters. With the snowfall blanking the landscape, the last of us took to the air. Only the Exit remained.

I hovered in front of the wall and saw myself reflected in a gray wash. Hundreds of players floated around me in the flurry, making their arrangements—which worlds they'd join, which people they'd become. Others zoomed past, already done with the game. A she-wolf and queen, tethered together, ping'd, */Kamikaze mutherfuckazzzz!* and entered the Exit. Their skins flared and sank into a molten afterlife. It took a full minute to be absorbed, their feet, their paws, the last to go.

Rrango dropped and found me. He was still skinned in koala, cigar and monocle and all, which looked ridiculous, but really that was what he'd given the Also—a sense that none of it mattered.

/been a great game o' golf, brother, he ping'd. */will miss you.*

I asked him where next, which alt.

/just landed a job dude. I need a life.

Everything was moving, at a barely perceptible speed, away from me.

/coming? Rrango ping'd. Half a square of grid remained, a

white strip between the Exit and the edge of Origin Park. The
end of the map. There was no more time. I had to let her go.

/yeah.

Rrango went first. He banked into the Exit, and it took
him. A sharp seam of light girdled his body as he sank. I'd
never hear from him again.

/Our turn next?

I spun around. Aremi, my prize, had dropped behind me,
finally. I told her I'd been worried about her, about what Melanak might have done.

/don't worry. am a big girl.

/there are other alts, I pulsed. /come with me?

I glanced over at the office door. Closed and locked. I
didn't want any interruptions—no Jocelyn to muddy the end.

/not sure, she ping'd.

/how about your email address?

/why?

/i want to know you better.

/ok, she ping'd back. /twat@faggot.com.

That's when I knew Aremi was gone. Her account, ghosted.
Melanak had torched everything.

/what the fuck do you want? I ping'd.

/hahahahahahahahahaha.

So I pushed her, all my damage-per-second arrayed against
her. Melanak tried to resist, except inside Aremi, he was a
weak soul. I would take her with me into the Exit and annihi-
late us both.

But as I drove her, the Exit began to retreat away, like

draining water. I chased it, Aremi struggling in my arms, but still it fell away, out of reach. Crowds of figures then emerged from the sky—iridescent dragons, armored horses, creatures I didn't recognize. Below us, a new render appeared, lush and vivid, pagodas dotting the land.

The Chinese platform. This was the integration.

/wtf? Melanak ping'd.

A dark-haired girl with black wings answered. / 什么性交？

/konichuwa, fucktard, Melanak ping'd back.

The girl raised her hands, whispered a spell, and a thousand crows came and tore us both to pieces.

I powered the machine down. I could hear Jocelyn on the back patio. I'd forgotten it was summer. I'd forgotten about the sun. Since Jocelyn was home, midday, it had to be a weekend. Outside, she was tending to the plants in a raised bed on our patio. She wore a straw hat, pink gloves, and a pair of cutoff jeans made from an old pair of mine, which meant, at some level, I didn't disgust her. At her side lay a small pile of weeds. She had tried so hard to make this place a place.

"It's over," I said. "More than over."

She removed her gloves and pulled me to her. "There's so much world left to see," she said, and let it hang there, between us, the line from the game, until I finally understood. "How about a tour?"

I got on my knees. I didn't know the name of a single plant in the row.

"Show me," I said.

Getting There & Away

On their first morning in what was the most spectacular place she'd ever been—rampant sun, palms everywhere, bungalows planked on top of the water—Haley and Mac paddled (Mac doing most of it) one of the resort's outrigger canoes to the raft in the lagoon (*lagoon, outrigger*, when would she get to use these honeymoon words again?) where, probably because he'd lost seven pounds since the ring sizing, Mac's wedding band just slipped off.

"Tell me you're kidding," Haley said. She sat upright, her left arm covering her breasts. She'd been on the raft, sunbathing topless for the first time ever, feeling pleasantly retarded from the mai tais they'd had at arrival the night before and then, because fuck it, again at breakfast. They'd flown for twenty-two hours, in a blur of deplaning and re-planing and magazines pulped down to their acrostics, to this crumb in the Pacific. She was not awake enough for an emergency.

Mac treaded water next to the raft, scanning the water, his snorkel mask askew.

"It's right below us," he said. "I watched it go." The ocean was pristine here. She could see forty feet down, to the ridges of sand that looked like the piping on corduroy. Bits of coral and kelp drifted in the current. But she couldn't see the ring, the white gold band they'd debated over forever that now had become, suddenly, a six-hundred-dollar piece of sea glass.

"Can you dive for it?" she asked.

"It's too deep. I tried."

Haley shivered. "Shit, Mac, someone could take it." Suddenly, the water seemed vast and rioting with threat. She thought of sharks and rays—the flappy mouse pad ones—and the Portuguese men-o'-war, which, she learned from the travel book she'd checked out from the library, were translucent brains with stinging hair.

"Mermaids might take it," Mac said. "For their merriages."

He was not nearly worried enough. "You're always in problem-solving mode until the moment I need you to be in problem-solving mode," Haley said, and worked her arms through the straps of her top.

Mac climbed onto the raft. "Hang on. Just let me boot up."

He lay down and whirred and clicked and sliced his hands through the air like a robot. Mac worked in advertising; he could only be serious after he'd riffed a little. Haley noticed the wet hair on his scalp made a land bridge from one side to another; the bald spot was progressing. The bald spot would need to be acknowledged and accommodated. His threadbare, beloved T-shirt (Madison High School Class of '99) was glazed to his chest; he wore it even in the water. He was shy about his scars on his belly, from a childhood surgery, but Haley felt, and she'd said something and then knew to drop it, that wearing a T-shirt while swimming made them both look like they didn't belong at the resort, like they'd won the trip on a game show.

"The ring's not going anywhere," Mac said. "I promise I won't take my eyes off it. But let me just say your breasts look fantastic right now."

"See, you just did take your eyes off it." Haley eyed the beachfront, the crescent of folding chairs and umbrellas. The other honeymooners at the resort, French girls with punky breasts who made Haley feel prissy for even bothering with a top, were nowhere to be seen. Last night, the place seemed overrun with young French newlyweds. She'd seen them all cramming into a hotel shuttle bus to the bars. But now the walkways that bridged between bungalows were empty. Haley untied the outrigger. She'd get help and she'd leave Mac out here if she had to.

"What the hell is that?" Mac asked.

And then Haley saw it too, the plume of black smoke in the sky, toward town. Something big was on fire. But they had other things to worry about.

In the breezy hotel lobby—it was a wind tunnel, open on both ends—the concierge gave Haley the worried expression she was hoping for. He had hazel skin, jet-black hair, and blazing white teeth, with a British flag pinned to the lapel of his white tuxedo.

"There are divers yes?" Mac asked, dripping on the tile. "We pay dollars. Many dollars."

When Mac said it, Haley realized she didn't even know

yet what the currency was here. Francs? Sand dollars? Mac's ring was probably worth a half year's labor. As soon as word got around that the ring was in the lagoon, everybody would be diving for it.

"No diving this day," the concierge said. "I am sorry."

"Not one?" Haley asked. "Not even, like, a guy with an air tank?"

"Tomorrow," the concierge answered. "Tomorrow, everything."

One of the French girls slow-walked through the lobby. She pressed a gauze bandage to her head with a crust of blood at the fringe. Too much fun? Haley thought vindictively. The girl's brown mane was clumpy and uncombed. She carried an ice bucket and barely picked her flip-flops off the floor.

"What happened to her?" Haley asked the concierge.

The concierge studied them both, as though this were a test of his congeniality. Then he handed her an island newspaper, a crudely printed broadsheet with all the weight of a shopping circular. "Beach Bombings Kill 23." Haley read the headline and saw in her mind the French girls thrown into the air, an explosion of brides.

Mac and Haley retreated to two rattan chairs to devour the paper. The previous evening, explosions had destroyed a restaurant on Jimbaran Beach, the tourist zone three miles up the sand. She tried to visualize the street. They'd taken the shuttle from the airport, through narrow streets of low-slung shacks and surf shops, with mopeds darting through every opening in the traffic. The route depressed her. Countless black wires crosscrossed above the road; did the whole island run off stolen cable? She saw the water in snatches between the buildings and eventually closed her eyes until they passed through the gates of the resort.

"Did you hear anything?" Haley asked.

"I thought I heard sirens," Mac said, but he often claimed special, unverifiable knowledge. Apparently, the bombs were crude, pipes stuffed with shrapnel and ball bearings, stashed in backpacks. None of the suspects had been found. The article said the majority of the victims had been islanders, and Haley allowed herself a small, guilty relief. The brides had been spared. On the second page was a photograph of a white man in a ruin of splintered benches and tables. Beside him, she could just make out a leg in the sand. A brown leg, without a person.

"Who *does* something like this?" Haley asked. Mac shrugged. She wanted someone to explain the facts to her. She was smart, she could hold it in her head, but this newspaper was toilet paper.

Bali had not been Haley's idea. She'd been thinking four-poster beds and long echoing halls of stone. Impressively, Mac had kept the honeymoon location a secret until the airport. Standing at the destination gate, Haley felt ambushed. In an instant, she knew exactly who had given Mac the idea. It was as though Saul had followed her here, into her privacy.

Saul was Mac's best friend from college, a curly-haired Virginian with a barking laugh and prominent chipped tooth that had somehow, despite his pedigree, eluded dentistry. Saul had spent a year island-hopping in Indonesia, lugging two surf-boards in a giant duffel. Five months ago, he'd returned to the States and crashed on their couch in Rogers Park to see if "Chicago was next." He was one of those people who appeared to live exclusively outdoors, on a mysterious trickle of cash. At different points, Saul had taught snowboarding, led wilderness adventures for deaf teenagers, built rustic log cabins for mil-lionaires in Montana.

"Will he make me feel pathetic for not having some amaz-ing life?" Haley had asked on the way to the airport to pick him up. She visited housing projects and patches of dirt she called "gardens" on all the forms. Her job for the foundation depressed her, would have depressed anybody, seeing that much rebar and broken concrete and kittens in tires. Often, when she pulled up to the curb, she'd have a moment of pure terror, when the idea of opening the car door and "leaving the bubble," as she called it, felt like a burden too great to shoulder.

"He can't make you feel anything, sweetheart," Mac said. "But I do tend to feel fat and pale around him."

Saul arrived in sandals and grimy cargo shorts and sick with stomach flu. He slept for two days. She found sand, fine as flour, on the bathroom tile. They left him the apartment during the day, and odd books, pilfered from their shelves, appeared on the counters. Haley and Mac came home to elab-orate meals Saul had made using every possible kitchen imple-ment. Cans of coconut milk mounted in the sink. More than one fresh pineapple lay quartered on the cutting board for them in the mornings. It was clear Mac loved Saul, or loved how Saul made him remember himself, but Haley found Saul's restlessness unsettling. She felt like he was going through every drawer while they were at work, looking for something they did not have.

Once, after a dinner Saul had made for them, Mac asked him about his walkabout in the South Pacific. Mac was good at making other people's stories interesting. Few people ever asked him about his work at the ad agency. If they did, he'd say, "It's all just a matter of deciding where to put the puppy." Mac hadn't traveled much, and as Saul spoke, Haley finally understood why Saul liked him—it was the same reason she did. He was precisely where you left him.

"So wait, where was that amazing beach again?" Mac asked from the bathroom, the door open while he peed. Saul brought out the insouciant boy in him. Soon, the cigarettes would be released from their cryogenic hold in the freezer.

"I'm telling you," Saul called back. "You two will not want to come home." He leveled his hand over the candle flame. "I almost didn't."

"But you did," Haley said. "You *did* come back."

Saul sighed and looked out the window. He'd tied his hair back in a ponytail. His features were big and American, a face that belonged on a coin. "You're right. And I'm still trying to figure out this whole slam." She understood Saul had lost the plot. Snow made drifts on the windowsills. Saul would not be staying in Chicago for long.

From the bedroom, Mac called out, "Hal, what happened to the goddamn atlas?" Because they still had an atlas. In fact, the whole Rand McNally set, spines unbroken, on the bookshelves next to the bed, Mac's contribution to the nostalgia fetish of their times.

She went to fill Saul's wine glass, but he put his hand over the rim and stared at her. "Is everything okay?"

She realized she had been avoiding eye contact with him, afraid of what he might draw out of her. It wasn't that Saul was beautiful. It was that he was utterly alone and had made a strength of it somehow, and that threatened her. She'd run from the solitude of her twenties, the stir-fries she ate alone, the solo trips to museums, the nights she called college roommates to check in. Mac had ended the anxiety, but it came with a sense that she'd avoided some essential encounter with herself.

"I'm fine. Why?" she said.

"Good," he said. "I wasn't sure. I want you to like me, Haley."

Of course she liked him. He was Saul's best friend. "It's just that sometimes I feel bad for not having adventures," she said. "Like you."

Saul just watched her. "I'm sleeping on your couch without a job," he said. "Welcome to the adventure."

The following morning, Mac off to work, Haley sat next to Saul on the couch to explain the television remotes. Saul, logy from sleep and wrapped in a sheet, took her hand and pulled her into a kiss. He was going to ruin her.

On the deck of their bungalow, Haley chewed her fingernails, nibbling away at the wedding lacquer. It was afternoon now and a busted upholstery of gray clouds rolled toward them at the horizon. The glassy lagoon stretched before her and water gently lapped the bamboo pilings underneath. From here, from the furthermost bungalow, Haley couldn't see another soul. Mac had gone to an Internet café—of course, they'd left all their devices at home except for Mac's phone, which had no bars, no network connection—to let their family know they were alive after the bombing, to look into the possibility of flights home, and she felt bereft. They'd paid for the remoteness, and now Haley desperately wanted others around.

She wondered if it was possible to keep these disasters from becoming the story of their time here. A friend had been married on a cruise ship in New York Harbor in the summer of 2001. Every single one of her wedding photos had the Twin Towers in the background. They were divorced now, and the only thing people saw was the wreckage to come. That must not happen to her.

While she watched, two brown-skinned islanders paddled out to the raft in an outrigger. They tied up and peered through the water. Haley drew a sharp breath. The taller of the two dove, his hands steepled over his head, and did not surface. Her chest tightened. They were diving for the ring.

Haley rushed along the walkway toward the hotel lobby, her eyes locked on the figures. She passed a hotel worker, a short, chubby woman. "Out there, bad things," Haley said, and the woman smiled warmly. Haley wanted to scream. At

the concierge desk, she banged the silver bell. The concierge
came wiping food from the corners of his mouth.

Haley pointed. "What are they doing?"

The concierge gazed outside, black eyes squinting. "These
men work in this place."

"You ask them to get our ring?"

"We ask," the concierge said, which wasn't even an answer.

Haley waited while he located a whistle. The concierge blew
it out on the deck and the pair paddled back to the shore. They
were both teenagers. The shorter seemed terrified to be noticed
at all. But the taller figure, the one Haley had watched dive,
was pretty and unafraid. His muscles looked like they had been
scored into clay with a knife. He was lighter-colored than the
concierge, almost caramel. Like the others, he seemed to have
no body hair whatsoever, a flawless envelope of skin. His age was
impossible to guess, maybe eighteen, maybe thirty, there were
no wrinkles to judge. Standing in wet swim trunks, he scanned
Haley as much as she judged him. She realized she was wearing
one of Mac's vintage T-shirts that read, "South East Asian Community Pride!" Please God let them not read English.

"What's your name?" Haley asked.

"Langy," the concierge said for him. "He only speaks Balinese."

"What was Langy doing out there?" she said.

The concierge translated. Between each consonant there
were these crazy, sweeping hammocks of vowels. "He say he
try to get your ring," the concierge said. "But he cannot find it."

"How do I know he doesn't have it already?" Haley asked.

It was an absurd question—he had nowhere to hide it—
but it felt appropriately skeptical and assertive. Haley watched
Langy's face for signs of nervousness. His cheekbones, she
wanted his cheekbones. Langy shook his head and spoke.

"What he say?" she asked.

"He say he doesn't see your ring."

"He say more than that," Haley said. "I hear more sen-
tences than that."

The concierge looked at her with annoyance. "Miss—" he
said.

"Mrs.," Haley said.

"Please calm," he said. "Your ring is where you leave it."

Mac returned from the Internet café with a warm bottle of
orange soda for her. He'd met a middle-aged Australian tourist
who'd been on the street when the bombs went off, who had a
cell-phone camera. The footage "was insane," Mac said as he
sat next to Haley on the foam mattress and tried, unsuccess-
fully, to recline on one of the odd triangular pillows.

"You watched it?" Haley asked.

"He seemed like he needed to talk," Mac said.

It turned out there'd actually been one blast inside the
restaurant, which killed some people, and when others rushed
outside, there was *another* bomb waiting street-side, a trap.

"Please stop," Haley said. "Are we getting out of here?"

Flights were booked for two days, Mac explained. Anyway,
now was the safest time, he said. "These things never go in
runs."

"You don't know that," she said.

"I do," he said. "I read *The Economist*."

"I never see you read *The Economist*."

"I savor *The Economist* on the toilet. Where you are not."

She told him about the staffers trying to dive for the ring. Mac thought she was paranoid. Nobody would try anything in the daytime, he said. Plus, the raft was right there. They could see it through the open doors of the bungalow.

He was doing his best to buoy her. He fetched two cocktails from the bar, tall glasses dressed with hibiscus flowers. He gave her a back rub that, inevitably, led to more. But even with the rum and slurry of tropical fruits in her, Haley was not in the mood. A pale green gecko moved across the wall above them. Everything seemed to be moving at the fringes, including the bungalow itself, rocking slightly in a breeze. Mac held her and napped. Haley looked out across the water and wondered what kept the raft in place, what deep cable made it stay.

In late afternoon, the clouds cracked and sent down sheets of rain. The power flickered in the bungalow for a moment and a volatile, blue-gray light rushed into the room. How fragile this place was, how jury-rigged.

"It's pouring out," she called out to Mac, in the shower. "The ring's going to get washed away."

Mac came to her in one of the big towels.

"What's the worst that happens?" he asked. "The worst is that we go and buy another ring." He thought for a moment.

"No, the worst is that I drown trying to get the ring back and you have to soldier on, the sexy widow, the WILF. Unable to love again."

Haley tried to pull away, but Mac reached his arm around her, intuiting her tension. Maybe other things got less beautiful as they got older, but his arms were strong and could hold her.

"Drowning was too much?" he said. "I'm sorry."

He convinced her to go to dinner off-resort, at a *warung* he had passed on his way to the Internet café. It was a classy restaurant, he said, with music and a guard out front checking bags and ID. Haley was reluctant to leave the resort, to join him on the rusting blue moped he rented. "You go to more dangerous places in Chicago, babe. You're totally hard-core."

"Is this the part where you mention Linda Hamilton?"

"This is not that part."

She got on the moped and discovered it didn't feel like imminent death, a bullet train to their bodies in a ditch. It was more like a restless carousel animal. When Mac cranked the pedals and the engine roared to life, she felt a swell of pride in him for seeming like he knew what the hell he was doing.

The road ran along a narrow causeway, beach on one side and marsh on the other. Along the roadside, roosters had been deposited in bell-shaped baskets, looking abandoned, watching the traffic. Taxis buzzed past them, horns beeping constantly. A warm breeze lifted Haley's spirits, softened the edges of her anxiety until another moped blasted past them with a "No Police" bumper sticker on the back. What could

that possibly mean? Who wouldn't want police? She belted
her arms tighter around Mac and stared out into the march.
She saw a small shrine, a gilded tower that looked like a dollop
of frosting, backlit by sundown. People came all this way to
meditate in a bog.

The restaurant sprawled off the side of a hotel, with tiki
torches flanking the front. The lot was crowded with cars and
motorcycles, which was a good sign—the place was popular. At
the entrance, an islander checked bags, but he waved them in.

"Great security," Haley said. "I feel really safe."

"Come on," Mac said. "I'm a white guy wearing jams right
now. I'm not scaring anybody."

Over speakers came the sounds of gongs and a woman's
voice wandering the scale. A mixed crowd of light and dark
faces filled the room. Haley felt reassured to see Westerners.
They requested a table far from the entranceway. The restaurant opened out to a patio at the back, overlooking the beach.
If necessary, Haley thought, that was where she would run.
When they sat, on chairs made from the trunks of coconut
trees, Haley caught herself in the glass of the table surface.
She wore no makeup and her long blond hair had gone viny
in the humidity. She looked like a woman who had stopped
showing up for things.

"Have I told you today how much I love you?" Mac said.
He clutched her kneecaps under the table and opened her
legs wide. "I love you this much."

While they were still working on their second cocktails—
these mai tais really were juicy and sinister—a waiter came

around with fresh fish on ice in a metal bucket, and they pointed out the pieces they wanted.

"When I went to the Internet cabana, I got an e-mail from Saul," Mac said. "His thing in Aspen didn't work out. He asked if he could stay with us again."

Saul's name plummeted inside her. He had left for Colorado and she hadn't heard from him, thank God, until the wedding, where he'd appeared in a red velvet suit. In the traffic of congratulations, Haley remembered hugging him and feeling his dampness, the sweat coming through the heavy material. In a flash, she remembered how much he perspired when they'd been together, the slick of his back. She thought he was over. She wanted him over.

"What do you think?" Mac asked.

"I don't think it's a good idea," she said.

"It wasn't a problem last time, was it?"

He held her eyes, studying her, and she felt like vomiting up the whole experience, get it out and get done with it. She had been waiting for the right time for the honesty, but it had not come, would never come.

"We need our space," she said. "And he's a grown-up. He can rent a place."

Mac nodded. "He was screwing girls left and right in Chicago, anyway. It'd be weird energy to have in our place."

The news gripped her throat. "Wait, he was?"

Mac took a big gulp of whatever oversweet garbage they were drinking. "What do you think he did all day?"

So Saul was a cad. That was not new information. And yet

she'd made the obvious error of believing she was special—if only so that it gave her power over him in her memory. Haley took Mac's drink and finished it.

The light in the restaurant dimmed, and someone turned up the music, which had triangles and gamelan and the sound of bamboo in trouble. Haley saw that islanders and grizzled sailors with scary tans now packed the bar. The women, in cutoff jeans shorts and miniskirts, had no hips. They snuggled in between the middle-aged Europeans, risking their fingers through the last redoubts of the men's hair.

"Are those girls?" Haley asked. "Or guys?"

Mac spooned up the last of the mango dessert. "Lady, if you gotta ask you're never going to know."

A striking brown-skinned woman entered, wearing a wig of perfectly straight, platinum blond hair. She eyed Haley for an instant before sauntering to the bar. She wore glass teardrop earrings, a dark blue dress, a cluster of loops at her wrists.

When the waiter delivered the bill, Haley asked about the men and their women at the bar.

"Yes, *waria*," the waiter said. "Bali specialty. Boy-girls. Pretty, yes?"

Haley stared at the blonde until she made sense. It was the tall young man from the hotel. Langy, the thief transformed. He wore nothing on his fingers, no ring, Haley made sure to examine the fingers. She watched as Langy shook hands with an older man with shaved brown hair, most of it on his neck, wearing Bermuda shorts and a tank top, criminal at his age. She stared long enough that, eventually, Langy looked back.

"Who wants to have sex with a transvestite?" Mac said, polishing off his fourth cocktail. "If you're straight, you want vagina. If you're gay, you don't want lipstick. Is every transvestite a lonely hag?" His head bobbed in the light.

"I think they just want to be beautiful," Haley said.

They paid the bill and Mac leaned on her to make it outside. He was in no shape to drive the moped. "I think I'm going to puke," he said. "I have that over-salivating thing." Haley led him to the shadowed side of the restaurant, near a dumpster. She stood by while he yawned up the fish and cocktails.

"It's probably sun poisoning," Haley said, rubbing his back.

Mac stared into his puddle. "Fucking sun."

Haley's eyes followed the sandy path that led behind the restaurant. She could hear the dinner conversations and laughter fanning out over the water and wondered if this was what the terrorists hated. The joy of paradise-seekers. Had their pleasure brought the bombs? What would be here without them?

Further up the alley, a shape leaned against the wall. She could make out the middle-aged man's Bermuda shorts even in the dark, halfway down his legs. At the man's waist, a head pistoned, hands stretching upwards underneath the Hawaiian shirt. Haley saw the blond wig, whisking back and forth. The man against the wall moaned and thrusted, holding Langy's head in place with both hands. The wig got out of place, and Langy, without stopping, brought a hand up to shift it back into place. The man sighed, pushed Langy off, and drew his shorts up.

A cab beeped in the drive and Mac stumbled off toward it. "Haley, come on, come on," he said.

Langy wiped his mouth and looked at Haley, straightening his wig. The older sailor passed Haley, head down shyly, beelining his way back into the restaurant, and Haley felt an exhilarating pulse of desire, of need, whatever it was that got her out of her head.

"Haley, *please.*"

In the cab, Mac leaned against the window, groaning at every turn. Haley opened his zipper and slid her hand in, holding him in her hand. She wanted to console him. He had just retched his guts out and still it stiffened.

"Oh, Haley," he said. "That feels so fucking nice but please don't."

She could have stayed with Mac, in the cabin, listening to him sleep. There was a guidebook that she had not read, had not even opened. But Haley felt restless and charged up, so she left Mac passed out on the bed in the bungalow, champagne tin at the side, in case.

Out on the lagoon, beyond the raft, a three-story cruising yacht had anchored. The lights through the portholes blazed across the water like low, close stars. A boom box played on the empty rear deck, a soundtrack of tinny pop radiating out and breaking the quiet.

Haley walked along the beach, past the neatly arrayed fleet of outriggers dragged up on shore. A handful of French couples had brought beach furniture to the edge of the surf, where they smoked and argued. She looked for the wounded one, from the foyer, but she was missing, maybe gone. Haley knew she looked suspicious, a newlywed alone on the beach, and she turned back up toward the entrance hall. A boy with a bag of laundry on his shoulder passed her. He kicked open a swinging door marked "Private," and before it swung shut she saw it led to a path into the palms.

This was it, the edge of the bubble, and Haley walked through.

On the other side, a short sandy path lead to a resort van with its rear door wide open. A shirtless Balinese man lay on a stack of white linen, nodding off. He righted himself when Haley stepped from the shadows, but she moved her hands to let him know that she didn't care. She tried to look like she knew where she was going. He rested back against the bleached sheets.

Haley came to a row of rooms, like a roadside motel. Ripped rattan chairs and small tables had been set on the walkway, with ashtrays on the ground nearby. One of the doors was open, and she peered inside at a thin cot covered with mosquito netting, a bedside table, and a television with the sound off. A blue waiter uniform hung on a clothes hanger, notched on the windowsill.

Somewhere nearby, a motorcycle approached and then idled. Haley backed around the corner of the building, out of view. At the far end of the walkway, a metal gate swung open. Langy, still in his dress and blond wig, stepped through, pulling his heels off his feet. He walked toward her and opened

the door to the last room on the row. She heard the crisp static
of fluorescent lights coming on.

It wasn't suspicion that led her to his door, but an odd curiosity. A sense that Langy still had something of hers. She spied
in on him from the open door. Langy sat on the edge of his cot,
his wig curled like a cat on his lap. He wiped makeup from
his face with a small towel. On the wall, he had pinned pages
from tabloid magazines, dozens of European models and ac-
tresses, at beaches and premieres and weddings, shot from
helicopters. It looked like the room of a teenaged American
girl. Haley couldn't recognize any of the faces. Europe really
had its own zoo of famous people.

Langy swanned toward a mirror and saw her, suddenly, in
the reflection. Without turning, with the delicacy of someone
who felt comfortable being observed, he smiled and waved
her in.

She entered and Langy pat the cot next to him. It
squeaked when she sat. Langy ran the back of his hand down
the length of Haley's hair, and then he took a brush from his
table and showed it to her, asking permission. Haley nodded,
not entirely sure what she was agreeing to, and then Langy
was combing her hair. As a girl, when her mother did it for her,
it relaxed her like nothing else could. Her mother would say,
"Tell me everything," and she would spill.

Haley closed her eyes and while Langy brushed, the story
came out. Saul, who managed to get her pregnant after fucking her twice. The nausea she had to lie to Mac about, and
her rage that Saul had appeared in her life so casually only to

come this close to detonating it. She just kept talking, about the clinic and cramps that followed, until what was buried inside her, this hidden awfulness, had been released.

When she finished, Langy lifted her left hand up to his face.

He peered closely at her wedding band. Then Langy turned to his bedside table and rustled through the drawer. It was teeming with jewelry—bracelets, necklaces, a jumble of glamour. He held his fist over her open palm and released a small loop of metal. A ring. White gold and expensive, but not theirs. Inside the loop was engraved for "my most beautiful —J."

"Where did you get this?" Haley asked.

Langy put his hands together and made a diving motion.

The boy, Langy's partner on the raft, entered the room breathlessly and stopped. In his hands he had a backpack. The top flap was open, revealing a row of metal pipes capped with duct tape. Langy leapt up and closed the flap. They spoke quickly and Haley understood that she didn't belong, had come to the end of the detour and was now risking her life. She wanted to leave, but Langy and the boy occupied the doorway, chattering angrily. Langy grabbed the backpack, more forcibly than Haley thought was prudent, and exited into the dark.

Crowds of other workers had already assembled on their patios when Haley left the room, and the presence of other worried people consoled her. They whispered and smoked and stared as Langy, still in his outfit, moved like a blue blaze across the grassy compound to another room. A man in a dress carrying a bomb—this would never end up in her story. He knocked on another door and the concierge, in a white T-shirt and hospital pants, answered, picking his teeth. This is how they truly were. Haley realized that she'd been looking at masks, seeing only docile supplication, from the other side of the reception desk. An argument grew between them, the boy shouting too, until the concierge spied Haley.

"What is happening?" Haley asked, trying to make her authoritative tone outdo her fear. He must know that, as a Westerner, she had access to news agencies, enterprises of scrutiny, an embassy window with a person who cared. Langy and the boy set the bag on the patio and backed away.

"The boy finds this," the concierge said.

"Where? Here? Tell me. In the hotel?"

The concierge did not answer, and instead held his hands in a prayer shape against his lips and tapped his fingers.

"It's a bomb, isn't it?" she said. She thought, So they do go in runs. "Tell me."

"Yes. He finds it in the lobby."

"You need to call the police."

The concierge took in the rows of workers watching her on their patios and balconies. His eyes seemed to sweep over the expanse of the apartments, not suspiciously but with a hard, unhurried sadness. She'd seen the same expression in the faces of families back in Chicago when she told them their plots of gardens would be cemented over for buildings, for development. The look of a bitter ending. Then it occurred to Haley: when the news broke, when she told someone that a bomb had been found here, the resort would suffer, their jobs would evaporate, detonation or not. This place would be over and she would be responsible for it. In an instant, the consequences tunneled out and away from her. Forget the ring. She and Mac would leave tomorrow on the first plane, back to what was theirs.

"Please go," the concierge said, and waved her off.

She walked through the gate and back into the foyer, then out to the beach, where a smaller, hardier circle of newlyweds continued to smoke. She folded her pants and blouse and walked into the calm lagoon. Nothing could hurt her out here. She swam out to the raft and lifted herself up.

The visiting yacht was nearby, and she could make out the bodies at the railing. They laughed at each other in a foreign language and leapt into the water. A woman in heels climbed down a rope ladder and fell. They were drunk, senseless, swimming at the boat's waterline, champagne flutes held in the air. Soon they would all know better.

The End of the Age Is Upon Us

Leah,

I forgot to tell you about the gravity + how I felt it! When we took the van this afternoon, just you + me, the whole way I heard a hum, like when you walk into the house + sense a television is on. Like electricity at the fringes. My container lifted, then pulled against the seat belt. It was the ship, at last, calling me, readying me for the jump. I wanted so badly to tell you, but wanting is a feeling, the hardest one to subtract. I looked up, but there were just clouds, dumb earth weather. The ship was invisible, just like Bo explained, tucked somewhere, in the tail of the comet.

Science proves there are all kinds of gravities. Moon ache makes tides. Even you, Leah, pull me. In two days, when the comet comes closest, we'll get on the scales + they'll say zero.

We drove to the university to post the Final Offer + it was strange because we saw brush fires in the foothills near the freeway. They made such a bright yellow hem in the hillside. I think California is going to die right after we do. Gray smoke drifted in the sky, the sun on a dimmer. As I drove, I stared

into the sun, dared it to blind me, but it didn't so I won. When
the snowflakes of ash flurried around the van, you weren't
scared because you had your Bible in your lap, the one that
you highlighted so much in yellow + orange + green marker
that it looked like the flag of some weird African country. You
tucked your feet underneath you, pushed your glasses up +
read from the unboring part. "I will show wonders in Heaven
above + earth beneath, blood + fire + vapor of smoke," you
said, "The Sun shall be turned into darkness + the moon into
blood." It was as if the Bible were a movie that we were watching + also living in, like costars!

The sky was scrubbed clean over the campus, perched on
the coast like it is. I parked in the lot at the student center +
paid the parking meter, even though soon there will be galax-
ies between us + our parking tickets. Inside the center, I was
surprised at how young the other containers were, younger
than us even, coral-pink + bronze, like they'd been buffed +
waxed + stored in a garage every night. I guess I've gotten
used to being surrounded by later models, like Old Margaret
+ Darwin + Bo. The students stared at us in our black turtlenecks. This made you anxious so I stared back at them until
their eye machines looked elsewhere. I wanted to shout, *Don't
you know what's happening? This planet is about to get recy-
cled!!!!!!!* But I didn't. It would take way too long to explain.
Besides, we didn't bring the overhead projector.

Instead, I took out Bo's flyer + pinned it to a bulletin board
that was quilted with countless notices of human irrelevancy.
"THIS IS OUR <u>FINAL</u> OFFER," the flyer read, in Bo's hand-

writing. "Civilization is about to be Spaced Under. UFOs will take us to the next level. Join us!"

You looked at all the flyers on the board + I asked what you were thinking + you said "nothing" + I said if you were having thoughts you needed to tell me, that that's what it meant to have a check partner.

"They have ballroom dancing on Thursday nights," you said.

Leah, you are so next level!

I remember how we found you street-side in Salt Lake City, with your retriever Rocket + your blond hair caked into rope. (It looks so much better short!) You were a seeker, your backpack crammed with books from every religion. You skimmed the *I Ching* + cast coins right there on the sidewalk, onto the front of your skirt. It took me an hour to build up the velocity to enter your atmosphere. Your facepart was so smooth + new. A hoop pierced your eyebrow. The two tiny bites into the skin looked maybe infected but still adorable.

I handed you our card.

Do you want to know what happens next? Come to a Total Overcomers Anonymous Meeting.

You cleaned a fingernail with the corner. "What happens next is you buy me lunch," you said + I took you to burgers. You left Rocket outside, tied to a banister with twine. You tried not to show your hunger, but your arm ringed the plate the way a gorilla would if a gorilla ate off a plate. I fell so hard for you, my knee bouncing under the table, even though I knew that was wrong + emotions add weight to our containers. You wouldn't

tell me about your life but now I know all about your life. Your
Mormon family, your brother who went AWOL on his mission
trip in Brazil + your mother who had an affair + how everything
splintered from there. I couldn't wait to rescue you, to give you
shelter + true family. I know it was awful when Bo made you
leave Rocket behind but that was a necessary shedding. Don't
tell me feelings are hard to give up! The most difficult thing
I've ever done was lie with you on that mattress + not touch
because Bo wanted us to "learn to be neutral." While we lay
there, every religion moved through me. If these letters can
prove anything to you it's that I've never been neutral.

At the student center, a male vessel got up from the entrance desk + approached us. "Excuse me," he said. "Are
you students? Because you need to be a student here to post
flyers." His vessel featured a brown ponytail + flip-flops + a T-
shirt that said "Alpha Chi or Die," which made me think that
maybe he knew something we didn't. A can of soda rose to his
mouthpart.

"This is very important for students to know," I explained.

"Well, there are rules and I'm the rule guy," he said. "Can
I see some ID?"

"Don't you want to hear about the Final Offer?" I said.

"This UFO *caca*?" he said + ripped down the flyer + crumpled it. That was when I realized we were talking to a Luciferian! Bo has told us so much about them, their ways of
scrambling our message, that I expected his eyes to blaze +
his lips to peel + show fangs. I really wanted to grab your container, Leah, + run.

"That was totally unnecessary," I said.

The Luciferian belched + his eye machines looked from me back to you. "And what's up with the twinky turtleneck get-up?" Then, to himself, he muttered, "California, land of the freaks."

"This entire world will end in two days," you said + it was beautiful.

Back in the van, we put our tuning forks to our heads + asked the Next Level what to do + I heard, "Return to headquarters." "Right now?" I said into the universe, but silently. "Can't I spend more time with Leah?" Then I swiveled my eye machines + saw you looking into the minivan beside us in the parking lot. The sliding door was open + those two twin babies, new vessels, fresh from the manufacturer, blinked in the backseat. Their mother bent over them + you waved to them in a tiny way. But the mother saw you + swung the sliding door shut.

"Finish your work," the Next Level returned, so I drove. According to my stopwatch, it had been one hundred + twenty minutes since we had launched from Rancho Santa Fe + we still hadn't picked up the fuel for the space jump. At the Ralphs, a cashier vessel with a bumpy facepart scanned our big jars of applesauce + cases of pudding + jugs of vodka. He said, "Looks like a party—can I come?"

I wanted to say, *The invitations were given out two thousand years ago!*

"The invitations were given out two thousand years ago!" I said.

"No need to shout, dude," he said.

"I wasn't shouting," I said.

"Lady," the cashier vessel asked you, "this guy doesn't have you against your will or anything, does he?"

You smiled + bagged.

But in the car, I could tell something was wrong. In the passenger seat, you watched the brush fires + hugged your legs to your chest. You left the Bible on the floor. I didn't say anything because I didn't want to bang your frequency. In the driveway, I parked + neither of us moved.

"Michael, do you ever have doubts?" you said softly to the dashboard. This close, your facepart was a sun that I couldn't look into.

"Doubts?" I said.

"Doubts about the Gate," you said. "About us going."

Leah: we all have spirits—memories + hopes + addictions + behaviors rattling around in our containers like sneakers in a dryer. They are the additions + we need to subtract them + get empty. My Spirit List is long: you, mainly, then my father then Boulder Colorado + my old programming job . . . These spirits make the doubts about the Gate + doubts are how the Luciferians win. They'll tether you here to the earth to endure the recycling. *To fit through the window in the sky*, Bo teaches, *you have to let go of everything that you are carrying.* Nobody said it would be easy to get the scales to zero.

"Spirits make doubts—" I said, but you said, "Never mind," + suddenly you were light years from me.

Inside the mansion, you walked straight to the Spirit

Room to decontaminate, which I thought was a good idea. We needed time apart. I took the grocery bags to the kitchen + hovered in front of the computers, each one blinking, "Red alert! Hale-Bopp is coming!" in an important font. I could hear Brian in the den recording his testimony for the video camera. Did you read his screenplay *Beyond Human*, which will change the world after we leave? It is 422 pages about Bo's emergency landing on the planet, how the away team created Jesus + the other vessels + what happens after the long war of earth living is finally over. It's so big Brian bound it with six-inch screws. Brian told me he came from Portland, where he made industrial films until his wife was mauled in a zoo-related thing. From the den, I heard him say to the camera, "Death is just the twist on page twenty-seven."

Bo was there in the kitchen, on a stool at the countertop, crushing our pills. I'm always honored to be alone in his orbit. It's selfish, I know—I get all his gravity that way. His silver hair bristled like a boot brush. I sometimes wonder what his face would look like if you smoothed out all the wrinkles—would it be the size of a tablecloth? Last month, Old Margaret whispered to me that Bo's vessel, the one he's been piloting for sixty-six years, is collapsing from cancer, which is why we have to leave now, while he's still strong enough to lead us through the jump.

When Bo saw me, he smiled. Then he said what he always says: "Such a beautiful container." Bo likes me more than the others, I think, because most of us have old containers or fat ones like Darwin's + Bo prefers the look of newer ones. I de-

cided this was the time to ask my big question: could I share
a bunk with you in the laundry room for the departure? "Yes"
would mean you + I would climb the sky together. I was so
nervous I was vibrating.

But Bo's face fell.

"Michael, your attachment to Leah is getting worse," he
said. "I'm very disappointed." It was as if he'd taken a hammer
to my container + pounded. "My answer is no."

I went to the laundry room + collapsed on my bunk, pulling big Gs of grief. I cried into my pillowcase for eight minutes + twenty-five seconds. I turned on the dryers to cover
my noise. I don't want to be alone, not for now, not for as
long as it will take to traverse the universe. Leah, am I with
you in the Spirit Room? Are you feeling the same? Are you
feeling at all?

When I was done leaking, I put the pillowcase in the washing machine with two cups of bleach. I got it clean.

Leah,

I woke up this morning + decided that I would not feel anything for you. When we all came together at 3 a.m. for our vi-
tamins, I took off my glasses so I didn't see you + swallowed in
the dark. During brain exercises, from 8:36 a.m. to 10:36 a.m.,
I finished my crosswords without thinking about you once. I
wrote our report about the human encounters from yesterday
+ didn't mention your questions or your doubts. At 10:54 a.m.,
I drank my protein formula + ate a cinnamon roll + more vita-
mins but I didn't look at your vitamin cup.

Then the doorbell rang + silence came. Darwin rushed into the den + said, "Someone's at the front."

A visitor! I got so excited because I thought it might be Jesus. Bo says that Jesus, the Total Overcomer, might surprise us one day but that he won't look like Jesus. He'll have a sheer face + black eyes + a giant head to hold all available knowledge. I thought of the last visitors we had. Remember those two Mormon missionaries? In their starched shirts + cowlicks, they asked Bo if he wanted to go to Heaven. When they saw all of us in our turtlenecks together, they thought it was a family reunion. "We're going to Heaven," Bo told them. "We're going to get there before you." We clapped in unison + the boys got scared like we were vampires + they ran away. I know you didn't like seeing them. You were thinking of your family back in Salt Lake + older brother, weren't you? Did he look like those two? Don't they all look the same?

Then I realized I was thinking of you again. I stopped myself by climbing the main stairs to see out the cathedral window over the door. I don't know why Bo let that one be the only window that is not covered with tinfoil. I think because it was too hard to put the tinfoil there.

Through the window, I saw an older female container chewing the pad of her thumb. Under her other arm she carried a cake on a plastic tray. She had long black hair + jeans + a winter coat, but there's no winter in San Diego so then I knew she came from elsewhere. Bo never mentioned a winter coat on Jesus.

"May I help you?" Bo asked when he opened the door. He was so thin now his white turtleneck hung loose on his vessel.

"I'm here to speak to my daughter," she said. "Her name is Leah Shearling."

"You daughter isn't here," Bo said calmly.

"How do you know?"

"There are no daughters here," Bo answered. "Only Overcomers."

She didn't know what to say to that! But then your mother peered inside, at all of us gathered in the foyer in the dark. It must be wonderful to see thirty-nine people with the same haircut + clothing, like the biggest math team that ever was.

"Leah, are you in there?" she called out.

I couldn't help it, but I looked at you, at the threshold to the living room. + the woman saw me look + followed my eye machines to you. You didn't make any expression go on your facepart.

"It's me, Leah. It's Mom," your mother said. "I want to talk to you."

"We have affairs to attend to," Bo said + started to close the door, even though all we had to do was more brain exercises. But your mother wedged her sneaker at the base of the door.

"I don't know who you are, or what this is about, but you can't hold her here," she said.

Bo turned to you. Everybody in the foyer cleared a path between you + him. "Leah, do you want to go with this human?" he asked.

I wondered if you would be strong enough to shed your feeling, right there in front of us. I wondered if I would be strong enough. But we have to let go + release even the best human memories. Like your mother. Like you + me, after the burgers. Remember how we walked up the ramp of the visitors' center in Salt Lake to the planetarium the Mormons painted there? We sat on the benches + peered up at the planets + you said, "I feel like an alien on earth, Do you ever feel like an alien?" So I explained about our vessels, how our souls drove them like cars until they were jalopies + how Bo would open the Gate for our souls to go weightless + level up. You'd heard so many explanations in your life you were skeptical. But your backpack was heavy, so heavy + confusing, wasn't it? The next morning, you showed up for our meeting in the hotel conference room. Then you went to that phone booth + looked up the name we told you + wrote down the place Darwin had written in the margin + came the next morning, to a field outside of town, where our van idled. You said, "I want to walk through the door of my life." Bo said, "This way."

But you came with Rocket on a leash. You had to leave him.

He chased the van until we got on the highway. You wept so much your facepart looked wet.

See, Leah, I do it too. Human love is remembering + remembering is the weight that will keep us here, on this dying planet.

In the foyer, I watched you shake your head no. Suddenly,

I felt warm in my chest, the way gas in the universe collapses
together + forms a hot star out of nothing.

Your mother broke down. She shot exhaust from her
mouthpart. Then she dropped the cake on the front step. Bo
closed the door + turned the lock + I could hear her crying
when we began to clap.

Leah,

Can I tell you something? When I was seventeen, I thought
maybe I was Jesus. I created my own religion where the saints
were the animals of my block. I believed the clouds of feeding
sparrows were the face of God. I composed psalms for the
squirrels on my clarinet. At this time, I slept in the basement
of my father's house, a house in a neighborhood of bullies, +
one night a gray tomcat came to my window. His emerald eyes
transfixed me. I let him crawl into bed, where he worked the
blankets on top of me + curled into sleep, his purr a throaty
rumble. This was my holy visitation.

During school, a new Bible wrote itself in the close-ruled
pages of my notebook.

Then one night, I found the tomcat at my window, dazed
+ bloody, one ear blown away to pink tissue. Bits of a fire-
cracker's red paper wrapper lay matted in his fur. He pressed
against the window screen but refused to come in, refused to
let me touch him. He had come to me to die. Have you ever
watched something surrender its vessel, Leah? I vigiled for
two days with water + food that this tomcat didn't eat until,
finally, his brilliant eyes shallowed + I was inconsolable, just

like you were with Rocket. I saw that our skin is an envelope, ready to be opened. My father thought I'd lost my mind. He called my mother in Phoenix for help. She asked to speak to me. "I have died for the smallest things," I told her. "Put your father back on the phone," she said.

I knew that the next time I found God, I would go with him when he ascended.

I told myself I would not feel anything today + then your mother came + now I feel again. All these possible worlds— every place, every person, is a planet, charging with life.

Leah,
It was midnight + tomb-time when I heard your steps outside. I rose from my bunk, peeled a corner of tinfoil from the laundry room window + saw you, at the end of the concrete path, past the tennis court + the dumpster, at the edge of the pool. I thought you were about to dive in, all dressed. But you stood still while the lights from under water—Bo liked to keep the pool lights on as a beacon for the ship—skittered across your body.

Why were you alone, without a check partner? I thought about Bo's counsel on the white board—"Major Offenses: Having likes + dislikes, Trusting your own judgment, Using your own mind" + I knew I had to rescue you from your thoughts. Which itself was also a thought but the right kind. I lifted the window + slid myself through it + snuck out to you because I wanted to know your secret. I wanted to be the one to hear it. I wanted to tell one too.

The bougainvillea flowers supernova'd into pink + red along the path. A warm wind brushed the palms. I came beside you + said, "What is it, Leah? What's wrong?" There are no mirrors in the house, but if there were mirrors you would be able to see how tired your eye machines were.

You said, "When you look up, what do you see, Michael?"

The clouds were gone + left a litter of stars. I was surprised that at night I still couldn't make out the ship or the comet, but Bo always reminded us that human eyes were foreign + cheaply made. I cranked my head back + laced your fingers with my fingers. It was wonderful + bad + strange since I had not touched someone else's skin for three years, since I joined up. Your container was so revved, like the hood of the van after one of our thousand-mile drives.

"I see our last night on earth," I said.

I had no thoughts when I kissed you except: I am not thinking, finally I am not thinking. I crashed through your atmosphere + landed in a place I already loved.

"What are you doing?" you said + pulled away. As you did, I could see Bo at the back door. His facepart was hard + cold under the door light, the way my father looked at me when he saw the tomcat dead at my window. Bo's gravity pulled us to him. Air pumped through his nostrils as if he'd come from a jog. His scalp was newly shaved but scored with nicks.

"Go immediately to your rooms," Bo said. "I will be there promptly."

What I didn't get to tell you: Leah, your mother wrote you letters too. Last year, when we lived in the earth-ship

made of dirt + Coke cans in New Mexico, her letters came
every month to our P.O. box + it was my job to check the
mail. "Christmas this year was lonely without you," she
wrote. "Daddy and I miss you and love you and hope you are
well, sweetheart. Please come home." There were dozens
of these letters, at holidays + birthdays + I learned so much
about you. They were even how I came to write these letters to you now. Once, there was even one all the way from
Brazil, from your brother. I got them + read them + I threw
them away.

Leah,
Bo almost found my letters to you tonight! He came in + told
me that the earth gravity has addicted me to human behav-
ior + that he wasn't sure that I would make the window any
longer. He searched my entire room—under the mattress,
my dresser, even inside my suitcase for tomorrow. (But not in
the lint filter of the dryer!) He knew I was hiding something
somewhere + that I was having my own thoughts. Then he sat
beside me + put his hand on my thigh + squeezed + said that
I would have to work as dispatcher tomorrow, which is like
doing the dishes except with people's containers. I wouldn't
get to see you at all.

I am still so nervous. I felt like I was about to shed in front
of him. He just left. Right after, I took out my tuning fork
from my pocket + consulted the Next Level but there was no
broadcast. I spent some time practicing my telepathy with you,
except you don't seem to want to transmit. I'll leave you alone.

Leah,

I'm writing you from the nursery, in the dark, because I don't have much time. This whole morning I have been running around the house like a crazy vessel. Helping fifteen people shed is not easy. Brian is supposed to be the captain but all he did was give me the plastic bags + tell me that I needed to make sure each person had eaten their medicine + shed their container entirely before going on to the next person. But that's hard because I'm distracted by you not being home + because some of the containers backfire + puke a little when they shed.

Old Margaret told me that you went with your new check partner Ladonna to get more applesauce (people had been snacking!). But you're still not home yet. It's almost noon. Where are you? Reading the greeting cards like you loved to do? Watering the plants in some parking lot?

I'm sitting here in the nursery because it was your room, because it is where babies were + they are weightless. I remember once we sat on the floor + you showed me your suitcase. It was covered in glow-in-the-dark stickers of stars. You had packed it with everything you wanted to take with you on the space jump: T-shirts + books + gum.

In the bunks around me, the four containers lay still, Thomas + David + Claire + Julie, because I already did this room. I figure they are at the ionosphere, maybe further. Their suitcases are next to me on the floor. Through the wall, I can hear Bo doing his testimony for the camera, the final one. "It is time to level up," he says. "The end of the age is upon us." I still have the fifteen plastic bags in my hand from the first departures. They have condensation inside them because breath becomes water when you shed inside them. I have to take them to the dumpster—Bo does not want us to recycle.

Writing this, I wonder how long the window in the sky will stay open + if we can still hold each other even if we cross through at different times or if that is just me being stupid. When I lived in Boulder, resurrecting computers, I felt I had no windows. Now there are many + they are open. Still, Bo says it is possible to miss our rendezvous + then we drift in the vacuum, like space trash. I have to stop now, somebody's knocking—

Leah,
I screwed up.

Brian came to the nursery. He had a whole bunch of messed up towels in his hand. He said he'd been cleaning up after me. "Why?" I asked.

"Just go upstairs," he said.

Bo + Old Margaret were clustered around the bunk in the guest bedroom. I knew I was in trouble. Darwin was stretched out, streamlined for his XXL container: hands at his side, Nike swoosh on his feet for velocity. Darwin was one of Bo's favorites. He had been with Bo for two decades. He even had his testicles erased in Mexico, like Bo had done, because of the drag. "Some students have chosen to have their vehicles neutered," Darwin once told the camera. "I can't tell you how much lighter it has made me feel."

Then Bo pointed to Darwin's chest. It rose + fell, rose + fell, a bad bellows. I must have taken the plastic bag off too soon, before Darwin was done shedding. Bo + Old Margaret stepped away + I knew my responsibility as dispatcher. I pressed my hand to his mouth + pinched his nose + stared at his chest to make it stop. But we all knew that I had banged his timing. Darwin is space trash now.

I felt sick to my stomach. I thought the insides of my container were going to come out my mouthpart. But Bo put his hand on the back of my neck. He said, "Don't take on his weight, Michael." All of the sudden, I remembered why I need Bo. Because Bo doesn't let any weight hold him to the earth at all.

Leah,
This is my last letter. I have to write it in my head because you're not back + I don't know how to find you. We're ready for the last group to make the space jump. That means me + you. Brian has bowls of pudding + applesauce along with baggies of Bo's powder. Plastic cups of the vodka we bought checker the kitchen table. I choose the applesauce because I think it will get you back faster. Old Margaret gives me a piece of paper that she printed with the Routine: "Eat two teaspoons to make room for the powder and stir. Then drink."

"Wait," Brian says. "Shouldn't we wait for Leah?"

Your name is a comet streaking.

Bo shakes his head. He'll be left behind to take care of

you, but that's not good enough. I want to be with you when we go. You are my gravity, Leah. The only way I can go is to follow you.

Everyone empties out of the kitchen in silence. We go to our rooms to eat our powder + drink their vodka + shed. My job as dispatcher is over. Bo remains in the room, gauging me. He knows how much waiting I'm capable of.

He blinks his eyes catlike + slow, the whole of understanding inside him. "It's time," he says.

I go mechanically, so without you, to the laundry room, to my bunk. The washer thumps with a full load. But I see that you've left me something! It's your suitcase next to the bed! I feel so happy. Even if you aren't here yet, I know that you will be with me, on the bunk above.

I set my applesauce + powder down. I go to the dryer to collect my letters to you. I wrap them in a shoelace + then I open your valise to sneak them into your belongings.

But your suitcase is empty, except for a page ripped from the Upanishads, something you could spare. "I'm not coming back, Michael," it says. "There is nothing in the sky."

Bo says that when a star explodes, it leaves behind the darkest energy in the universe. My eyes leak, the last of what's inside me. This is what it took to get me to zero.

Bo is at the door. He spoons my dose into my mouth. I don't stop him. The applesauce tastes bitter + gritty, like ashes in mud. Bo pushes me flat, so I rest, his hand brushing my cheekpart. Then, I hear the hum, soft at first but soon it is in my jaw, like my head is pressed against the generator of the ship rending space. Leah, vanisher, you will never know this. When you look up, you will not see us, not the comet only the tail. Not the thing only the going. Then the hum shatters my container, the hum is the blood in my ears + it slows + slows + now Bo with a plastic bag in his

The Worst You Can Imagine Is Where This Starts

The bag looked all wrong, tucked against the wall of the basement near the root cellar, glistening under the bare bulb.

Graham knew he hadn't put the bag here, and Graham was the only one in the family who put anything down here. The place was a warehouse of his unfinished business, the tool table an open grave: lobotomized light switches, hopelessly knotted crowns of Christmas lights, the radial saw whose cord—the fucking brain stem!—he'd chewed through on the first go.

His wife, Marlena, would venture down into the basement only under duress, in desperate sorties, with a broom in hand to mash spiders. In fact, they now had a special broom just for mashing spiders, the tiny berries of their carcasses poleaxed on the straw. (It lived, unspeakable, at the bottom of the stairs.) Their sixteen year-old daughter, Emma, deemed the basement "sketchy" and also "rapey" and refused to come down. There was a lot of refusing left in her, Graham was learning. So the basement was his alone, to clutter and abandon and befoul. But then, here was this black contractor bag that he had all of nothing to do with.

Graham set down the space heater he'd come for, feeling put-upon. He'd taken a personal day for a morning of triage. They were selling in the spring, if they could get a buyer. If the market didn't shit itself again, if he could get this base-ment cleaned and maybe paneled and deem it a room. He'd work until Em came home for lunch—most days, she bolted from school, what she once called "the hellscape." They would have a wary, silent lunch together like strangers at a cafete-ria, Em's head down, not making eye contact, eating a grilled cheese he'd make for her, and scrolling her phone for a drip of validation.

His attention went to the open window. He remembered Marlena saying that she'd opened them to "let the must out," *must* being whatever made their clothes smell ripe and sub-terranean, though Graham believed (it wasn't worth the argu-ment) that the open windows let the must *in*, that the must was inside the house, a part of it now, generations of sweat on the wood. But they were selling soon. It would be someone else's must.

Marlena had found three grassy, charmed acres at Five Mile, outside Grand Rapids, where they'd build. It was their dream, their best-case scenario. They were on the verge of themselves. They had Emma young, and Emma had been hard. First night terrors, then quaking shyness, and most recently weeklong silences to punish them for their interest in her life. She treated Graham like he was a parole officer, sensing judgment in her every move, and offered glimpses of her personality only when she wanted special dispensations. She had one friend, a redhead named Helena who said nothing to them, ever, a statue with freckles whose parents were divorcing and left her needy, and together they could vanish into black holes of time. At last, though, Em had come into a boy period, and what self-immolating energy that consumed her now found direction. Already, two different boys with inky hair and piercings had come to the door for her, and the horizon of her departure from their daily lives was in view. Graham and Marlena had spoken to an architect, even rolled that appointment into drinks for the two of them. The silhouette in Graham's mind: a wood-timbered ranch with a raked slate roof, floor-to-ceiling windows on the side facing the grasses, obscene amounts of light . . . He would tell Josh and Delia at work that after two decades ferrying copy and deliberating offsets, he'd get to know every joist and stud in the house personally. His hands would finally get dirty.

Graham's attention circled back to the bag. Someone fleeing the police had thrown it through the window, he decided. There were drugs inside it—he imagined a Tide-like mound of cocaine. The neighborhood had tipped, hadn't it? A few weeks ago, a rental property up the street had its porch set on fire. Their next-door neighbor, a young plumber named Aaron, had just adopted a German shepherd "for protection," an animal now digging holes under their shared fence and barking neu-

rotically at squirrels. Graham and Marlena moved in when Em
was just two, when the area was up and coming. But it never
quite came. An alarm company had come through and he'd
noticed their neighbors all had the signs jabbed into their front
flower beds. Every window, every door, wired. Marlena had
refused. "I don't want to live in a terrified world," she'd said.

But the window, Graham saw, was intact, the screen in
place. So the bag had been placed there from inside.

Graham picked it up. Something inside was dense and
jointed and uncocaine-like. He set it on the tool table, and
undid a knot in the plastic. A fetid smell gusted out, enough
to make him recoil.

Later, that dark bloom of plastic, opening in his hands, was
what he could not stop thinking of: the moment *before*, when
he had the choice to stop, to tie it up and fling it into the trash,
and never see the corpse. Inside the bag, the baby was facing
down, almost deferentially, its back to him. It was a mercy to
have not seen its face. The skin was still speckled with birth.
Graham would remember the ashen color and the scale of it,
six months along, too small to be full-term, for the rest of his
godforsaken life.

He walked over to the slop sink and heaved. His hands
closed the bag, shaking convulsively, and cinched it with a contractor tie. His thoughts spiraled into thinking about Em, this
stranger who was his daughter. How could they have missed
the months of her showing or the sickness—Marlena had been
bedridden for months with her—or the advances of one of her
pierced suitors, these friends with benefits?

Graham couldn't leave the bag on the table, or the basement floor. He didn't want it to touch anything in the house, to deposit a residue of itself on their lives. He gathered himself, by some ancient instinct, and walked out into the backyard.

The air was frigid, biting, even at noon. He could see the top of their neighbor's white plumbing van over the fence. Graham stepped into the shadow of his garage, out of view, and laid the bag softly (how else?) on the hard-packed ground. It seemed vital to get the bag in the ground before Graham thought too hard or too much. He needed a shovel. If he dug deep and quick, the fact of it wouldn't take hold. Before Em, back when Graham and Marlena traveled the country—they were hoboes for a couple of years there—they had a running joke: when things got bad, when they'd left some shameful evidence of themselves somewhere, he would rush into the car and say, "*Go, go, go!*" like a getaway, like the end of a heist, because you recalled a place less the faster you left it.

He left the bag and stepped into the garage. The wall had one empty spot for the shovel, next to the rake and the broken rake and the pitchfork that was a prop in some life he would never live. Then Graham remembered Aaron at his back door over the weekend, his presidential face, dressed in a thermal shirt and grimy jeans, shovel pieces in his hands. He said his shovel had snapped when he'd tried to attack a tree root. So he'd come through the door in the fence between their yards—installed by their prior neighbors, who imagined a community on the block and then promptly relocated to Houston—to ask to borrow theirs. Facing him on the back stairs, Aaron peeked around behind Graham, at the kitchen interior, and said, "Hey, Emma," and Emma, at the island, smiled, and Graham wondered which men earned her attention and which her dismissal. In the yard, Aaron's German shepherd, improbably named Schatzi, ran around, sniffing, pissing on the sapling Marlena had planted. Graham recalled the swell of masculine provisioning he felt escorting him to the garage, where he handed over his own shovel. Keep it as long as you need it, Graham said, while Aaron surveyed his wall of tools, his whole garage, as though he might find another tool he wanted.

Graham noticed a trowel in an empty flowerpot. It had a sparkly red handle. Marlena had bought it for Em, her *very own trowel*, to encourage gardening, though Em preferred to do anything but. Now that he thought about it, where had Em *been* yesterday? Or the day before? Graham's thinking hit the wall of her routine: school, dinner on the couch, then up in her bedroom, earphones in, computer on and trilling. When did she look up long enough to *get* pregnant? God, he barely knew her.

He took the trowel grimly, knowing a bad decision the instant he gripped the handle.

He chose a spot near the pine tree, screened by the fence from the rear alley. The ground was dense and dry—Graham had to jab with two hands. The dirt made a pitiful pile until he reached sand a few inches down. He could hear the shepherd next door snorting in Aaron's yard, pacing the fence line. Don't bark, Graham willed. Don't.

He'd done this once before. One summer in high school, he buried the family cat, a beloved throw pillow named Moe that had never quite understood that the road outside the house was a goddamn killing field. He buried her in the ground and surprised himself weeping inconsolably at the graveside, kneeling against his mother's leg and discovering it was sweet and perfumed and cluttered the grief. The next summer, their neighbor set a fence and drove a backhoe into the ground right through the plot. That would not happen here.

Finally, a hole opened up. Deep enough, he thought. Graham set the bag in the hole and tucked the extra plastic in. It occurred to him that inside the plastic, nothing would rot. Generations on, you could dig this thing up and know just what was inside. He got the pitchfork from the garage and jabbed into the bag. The tines struck soft matter and he willed himself to think no further. Then he kicked dirt on top and tamped with his foot, delicately. He promised himself he would never tell anyone where this was. This was the absolute final time he would allow his eyes to fall on this spot. He was murmuring a half-remembered prayer when his cell rang inside the house.

It was Marlena, at the library. He found himself at the counter, phone in hand, unable to answer. If he moved, if he answered and so much as spoke the events of the last fifteen minutes aloud, a crack would spider its way through their entire lives. No one could know. If he called the police, Emma would go to jail, or he would. That is what happened in an area like this, where the pro-life ads on billboards—fetuses, forty feet tall!—promised good lives and loving parents to every single baby if you would just allow them into the world.

He let the air run out of his lungs. The phone went silent, and in the silence, he discovered he needed Marlena to know. She would know which lawyers to call, how to sit Em down and not destroy her. She worked at the branch library. She could parry anything.

She picked up at the first ring.

"I found something," Graham said. "In the basement."

Marlena sighed. "Did the sewer explode again? Because we're staying at a hotel this time."

"No, it's not the sewer. You need to come home right now."

"Tell me what's going on."

He looked out through the kitchen window. A strange shape moved out by the pine tree. Dirt kicked up in the air. He saw the shepherd's black muzzle nose the grave.

"Get home," Graham managed to say before he hung up.

As soon as the screen door slammed behind him, the dog turned and gripped the ground. A low growl escaped from its tawny throat and then a single bark ripped through the air. Graham froze, empty-handed. Schatzi's black eyes did not waver.

He could see the trench at the far end of the fence where it had, finally, dug underneath. He had to get the dog back on other side, either through the door or the gap it made.

Aaron would hear the barking and come. He had to undo time. Graham stepped backward and his hand fell on the stem of the pitchfork, resting on the back banister.

At the grave, he could see the black plastic shredded already. He had been wrong—he could never hide or forget the fact of the burial. It was a sinister molecule in the universe, pulling things toward it, like his family, his future, like his right foot, moving one step forward, which shattered some invisible perimeter around the dog, and it dove forward and snarled.

Graham held the pitchfork out. Schatzi snapped and backed up. Graham went to the door in the fence and flipped the latch. It swung open and the dog's ears pricked up, quizzically. Now, Graham edged in wide circle to the opposite flank.

"Come on, come on," Graham said, trying to settle him, making eye contact.

Schatzi rotated with him. Graham's two hands held the pitchfork out, his only defense. When he took a step toward the hole, the dog lunged. Impulsively, Graham thrust. The tines of the pitchfork jabbed once, into the dog's fur. Schatzi yelped and reeled away toward the fence, where Aaron stood in the opening, mouth agape.

"Jesus Christ," Aaron said, leaning over to grip Schatzi's collar. His hand came away smeared with blood. "What the fuck?"

The screen door to the house slammed. Graham felt a wave of relief. Marlena was here. Marlena would know which lawyers, everything.

But it was his daughter, Em's face contorted in horror, and

redheaded Helena, Aaron too, these witnesses, every one of them seeing him and the pitchfork and the gray limbs exposed to the air. Graham could not move.

"Everyone, please, go back inside," Graham said.

Then, in a kind of trance, Helena stepped down the stairs. She wore tight, ripped jeans and a sweater that looked collapsed. Her face had spots where she picked at it. She walked straight past Graham and fell to her knees at the side of the grave, the black plastic visible. The German shepard barked and tested Aaron's grip.

"What did you do?" Aaron said, staring into the hole.

Helena looked at him, bitterness etched in her face, Aaron's face went slack in recognition, and she began to rake the earth into the hole with her hands. Graham dropped the pitchfork and led Em inside, *Come with me*, where they looked at each other across the kitchen island, both of them shaking, trying not to hear the low voices outside. His daughter's eyes were imploring, terrified, and he realized he had grown accustomed to not seeing them, not knowing her. Em tucked her hands into the sleeves and he told her to tell him what she knew, what had happened in the basement, and then they would bury the details and, together, never say another word.

The five acres at Five Mile will not be theirs. The market will shit itself again, but they will sell their house and buy another house. Em will go away to college, but she will call regularly, and when she calls, she will ask to speak to her father because, and this he couldn't have predicted, she will want him to know her. The event of a secret will become a kind of gift. She will tell him about strange boys she meets, about her anxiety, about the place she volunteers. Eventually she will talk about traveling, as her father and mother did once, to ruins in Asia, to the coast of Spain, gathering distance from them and from the dark molecule. And when Em does, Graham will hear his voice, across the years, saying, *Go, go, go.*

Ledge

Mother, I have seen such marvels. Like the ocean aglow at night with a cold green fire and a fish with a child's face and two fleshy whiskers. (No man would eat it. We blessed the creature and tossed it back.) I've seen a corpse with golden hair in a boat set adrift; his eyes were the slits on a newly born kitten. When the boatswain came to after three days on the *garrucha* for the crime of sodomy—his wrists tied behind him and hoisted above the deck so that his arms tore and jellied—he asked, "Am I dead?" and soon he was. I looked to Diego, who dropped his dark eyes in shame, and I saw that too. Three hundred leagues into the sea, we came upon a floating meadow, crabs and petrels tinkering along its dank branches and fronds. A palm tree had taken root there and I imagined, briefly, the coastline of Seville, of home.

But none of these compare to you, Mother, suddenly here, at the gunwale of this ship, soaking wet. Your hands are folded across your chest and you stare away, at the ledge. You look precisely as I left you, your long black hair damp and loose against your back and your bare feet white as salt. Around me, the crew and the others race to trim the *Elena*'s sails in a westerly. The captain is missing and I am full of questions. Are you a dream?

Is this a fever or worse? I'm afraid to speak. And so I sit alone with my ledger, in the shade of the quarterdeck, and write.

The great Venetian saw the court of the Kublai Khan and wrote his *Book of Marvels*. I remember how I loved it as a young man, how I stole into the college to read the manuscript and teach myself the words. It took me a year to finish it, and when I was done, I started over again. At night, I dreamed of trader Polo's adventures: the falcons of Karmania, the gold and silver tower of Mien, and the festival of wives. Marco Polo told his story from a Genoese jail. The *Elena* is now my prison. His stories saved his life. Perhaps so will mine.

This record began three days ago, on the *Elena*'s twenty-second day at sea. We sailed in search of the sea path to India, driving a slant from the Canaries to the Azores into the blue-black unknown. For days, we had been mired in a meadow of sargassum. Captain Veragua, convinced it was the grass of a submarine ridge, ordered the crew to sound the waters on every watch. But the bulb of lead, at the end of the fathom-long cordage, could not sink through the dense thicket. In boredom, the English conscript used a crossbow to hunt a petrel, resting on the carpet of weed, and his arrow succeeded only in punching it down into oblivion. But on Sunday, the meadow miraculously began to break into patches and then lacy fingers. As it trailed into our wake, the crew sang psalms and "Salve Regina" with renewed (if not exactly pleasing) vigor.

Summoned by our good feeling, a group of dolphins as-sembled beneath the *Elena* and moved together like a shadow, fracturing and collecting with astounding speed. They teased us, the way children at the Magdalena city gate greet strangers. They leapt into the air and made an exuberant birdlike speech. I opened the navigation ledger and stared at our rhumb line, fixed at one end and one thousand leagues long. I wrote, "Sea like a river, new company, new hope."

And then a cry came from the rigging. Diego, swung up in the web of mainsail rope, yelled a shapeless sound and pointed frantically off the side of the ship. At port, two iridescent coils, the height of three men, arched across our length. They moved as fast as a lash and seemed pure muscle, strong enough to splinter the *Elena* to matchwood. Their scales shimmered like slick cathedral glass. I froze with the ledger open on my lap. Before long, other sea serpents, large as the first, foamed the water in a frenzy. The ocean was a tipped basket of eels. The serpents coiled and, at once, lunged beneath the boat.

The men backed away from the gunwale. The waters went still and the air flashed with heat. No man moved. In short time, our wake ran red. Bits of pink meat floated and were snatched down.

Pinzón, our interpreter, clutched my arm.

"*Where*," he whispered, "*are we?*"

Every sailor knows the stories of sea cats and mermaids with cadaver-cold breasts. St. Brendan told of riding on the back of a whale. But in my young years at sail, as a scribe, men never died from stories. They reefed on fogged-out coasts. They wrecked on breakers off Cape Bojador, circled forever

in the Mare Tenebrosum. Except now, new horrors brushed
against our keel and knifed the water. We were eighteen men
buoyed by forty feet of caulked and tarred oak, a thin wooden
wall between our fate and us.

Thirteen-year-old Marco, the ship's boy, squirreled up the
mast, as high as he could go. The brothers Alfredo the Tall and
Armando the Taller fell to their knees and raced through the
Lord's Prayer. Others went to the sail locker for armaments,
but the *Elena* is an ocean exploration ship, fast and weak.
We carry no arms stronger than crossbows and a meager fal-
conet mounted on the deck that spits spoons and scrap metal.
Against raiders—or worse—we have little defense.

Only Diego bravely craned over the side and searched
through the water. I wanted to go to his side, the safest place I
know, but panic fixed me.

"What do you see?" the English conscript said to him,
teeth clacking. Piss had spilled down his right legging and his
swagger had gone with it.

Diego did not reply. He had his tongue and his wit but was
as mute as a fish. Much as I felt for him, Diego has never spoken
my name. Can you love something that you never name?

We found him grinning on the steps of the cathedral, a
drunk Franciscan friar, tonsure gone prickly. A spray of freckles fell across the bridge of his nose and vanished under whiskers, his face an admixture of boy and man. The friars said
that he'd been silent since he entered their order and had
never taken to cloistered life; instead, he kept the garden full
of flowers that brought the birds, then the cats, until a plague

of aphids finally brought it to ruin. He was round as a cask and the captain, searching for crew, asked him to join us as a cook, pointing down to the banks of the Guadalquivir, to our expedition ship, with her royal flags sharp in the wind. Diego's gaze went out, past the sails of the barques and the harbor riot, toward an unseeable shore.

How is it that some men inspire no feeling in me while others stir the deep waters? On those cathedral steps, I took his right hand, smooth as calfskin, and he pressed his left against the outside of mine, so that my hand was held in a gentle, warm prayer. I felt my blood rise up, the way a bulb of quicksilver feels in a pot of boiling water. He pointed to my ginger hair and made a flickering motion of fire with his fingers. I smiled like an idiot. And if Diego did not speak, his hands were more fluent than any words. He practiced a religion at the cook box, the communion of salt pork and sea fish, all that mattered. And at night, in shadows, those hands made other blessings. Now, at the bulwark, Diego looked eager and expectant. As if this encounter was his whole reason for coming.

The deck bell rang. Captain Veragua came to the entrance to his quarters. In the daylight, he was plainly dying. He wore a hood, white eyes shining from the shadow like marble. On our second week at sail, the captain had stupored on wine and a candle in his cabin tipped in a swell, setting his bedclothes and doublet alight. He jumped overboard and when he was fished from the water, his left side looked like a hank of meat rescued from embers. It took two days for Diego to pare the seared cloth from the captain's skin with a carving knife. Every command he gave to us now was curt and purposeful, trimmed to the minimum amount of gesture.

"Peralonso," the captain asked me, "what is that sound?"

My attention went to the sails. The wind had worn out; the main and the fore drooped without breeze. The ship's planks creaked in complaint. The sea slapped lightly against the *Elena*. We had entered a white calm, the horizon crouched behind a mist. But as I listened, below all of this came a faint, wide roaring, like the rumor of a waterfall. It stretched the width of my perception.

"Land?" I answered.

The captain ordered the deep-sea lead hove overboard again. The lead, at one hundred fathoms, failed to find bottom. The brothers recalled the line, spliced a second to the first, and sent that into the sea. Again, the rope drifted behind in the current. The sea was too deep to sound.

Then the captain called for the crows to be released. They cawed up in their cage, high on the mast. Marco scampered up the rope ladder and released them. The birds circled higher and higher, hunting shoreline. As land birds, they hate travel over seawater. But they continued to circle until we could not make them out.

"Listen," the captain said.

Soon enough the drone was all I could hear. The *Elena* drifted in a weak current. Slowly, as the world reaches focus through a looking glass, the mist thinned and revealed itself as a great spume of ocean water. One league away, the curve of horizon straightened to a line, to a drop, like the edge of an enormous table. Clouds bent over this line and disappeared.

Coralito, the *Elena*'s frail navigator, crossed himself and went to the captain, our sail chart spindled in his hand. He was an old and difficult man, a widower, too vain to admit his fading eyesight. Long white eyebrows billowed from his face, like puffs of sweet weather. But aged as he was, Coralito was the *Elena*'s will, our human compass. At the Talavera Commission in Salamanca, he watched Queen Isabella decree, on a carpet of maps, that the world was a plate ringed by water and that to traverse this lip from Spain to the Indies would take three years. Under his breath Coralito had muttered, *What do priests and Queens know of science? The world is not flat, but as round as a ball of wax and as knowable. You can leave a place, travel a line, and arrive where you began.*

"What did you say?" the captain asked.

"I have failed you, Captain," Coralito said. "I was wrong."

The crows returned and settled noisily on two belaying pins.

"We have reached the edge of the ocean," Coralito continued. "We can go no further. This is the fourth corner of the world."

Every man is born to his first corner. Mine was a pile of flour sacks in a house in the port of Seville, in the year 1469, under the reign of King Ferdinand of Aragon. That year, my father, a blacksmith, was conscripted into the *armada marvallosa* in the English war and lost at sea. He returned to my mother as one thousand *maravedis* of wheat grain, the compensation for her sacrifice. Desperate and poor, my mother bricked in his furnace, hand-ground her grief into powder, and opened a bakery.

Every morning, I rose to find her kneading the dough, and I will always remember her ghosted with this fine white dust, cool and papery to the touch, haunting a passage to and from the oven. She was a striking, sad beauty, her hair gathered in a silver band. Countless men needled me in an effort to get her attention and force a smile on her. But none could tempt her out of the downward stare of her solitude.

"You must never leave me," she would say, flattening my hand against her cheek. "One day you will want to. It will be a girl with gray eyes, or a distant shore. That day, you will count all the things that are keeping you here and they will not be enough. That day will be my last."

My mother gave me the gift of letters. When I was thirteen years old, she led me to a field of goldenrod and covered my head in a shawl. She told me I must study a new book and make new prayers. I asked, "Who are we praying to?" and she said, "To the God of Israel, your true people." That afternoon, I became two: a Catholic, the faith of my father, and a *Marrano*, Jew by candlelight.

Soon after, the butcher came on afternoons to sit me on his lap and write letters on a slate. He read the words aloud while I repeated them. Sometimes he would whisper made-up words in my ear, or put my hand on his belly to show me how breath worked until he sighed. I delighted in this, but my mother sent him away. "You're too old for such things," she said. I wept inconsolably for a loss I felt but couldn't bring into words.

Over time, my mother's bakery grew to serve the harbor, preparing tack and meal for sea journeys to and from the Levant, the terminus of the spice road. It was my task to deliver the breads to the *barcas* and *navículas* anchored in the river. I grew to love the crowded port, so dense with ships that I could hardly see the water. There were many familiar faces, salted in every crease, and crabs savoring the treacle on drydocked hulls. The port felt like a floating city of fathers: exuberant, bronzed men, barefoot and dressed only in trousers. They taught me knots, the mysteries of splicing and parceling the cordage, even as they pilfered my breads. Many asked if I wanted to join their crews, but only if I could assure that their hardtack would never worm.

I was tempted. The sailors spoke of the Spice Islands, the Moluccas, and their incomprehensible bounty. They had seen the moon dyed orange by windblown curries, palms scorched betel-red. Along the coastline, the air was so heavy with pepper you had to breathe through cloth. It seemed to me that these spice villages harvested delirium, and the lives there were surely made of pure color.

Once, the boldest I ever was, I stole into the hold of a docked caravel. Twenty barrels sat lashed to the floor. One barrel had been knocked open, revealing a rubylike powder. Mace, the fine netting on the nutmeg shell. I'd seen it in the market, a spice so treasured that a tablespoon is worth a week's labor. I tasted it with a finger. I felt that I was savoring a quality of dusk.

Just then, a mariner stepped from the shadows. He was broad-shouldered and grimy, as if he'd been swimming in the bilge. I stumbled back, afraid. He motioned for silence and slid closed the lid of the barrel. From the deck, I heard the mainsail catch in a gust and felt the ship pull.

We stayed that way, in stillness, until I broke free and launched myself out of the hold. Seville was already some distance behind. The crew, surprised by a stowaway, laughed at my terror—I'd never gone to sea, never learned to swim. A hand shoved me overboard, into the water, and I could hear their pleasure at my thrashing. The shoreline disappeared from my view, and I was sure to die.

Without warning, a thick arm wrapped around my neck and I found myself dragged to the surface, then to the riverbank. I vomited water into my lap. My rescuer, the man from the hold, stared back at the ship as it coasted down river. Our swim had transformed him, washed him clean. How supple and pale his skin was, with inky hair tufting along his arms. He took a bandoliered wineskin out from under his shirt—the cork had popped and the wineskin was swollen with water. He poured it and the water ran clay-red. The stolen, ruined mace. The thief shook his head and tossed the skin into the current. We said nothing.

I brought him back to my mother's shop. My mother was gone and we lay on my bed of flour sacks to dry. He held me tightly, his arm belting me from behind, as Diego has done, as if I were on the verge of falling. There are many ledges that split this world, between the known and the unknown, and we choose to go over. While the thief slept, I watched his pulse tick in a vein in his forearm, a single cord snapping taut then loose in neat, regular meter. I was more awake than I'd ever been. It is said the celestial spheres chime as they roll against each other. In just this way, my body vibrated against his. I knew then I would leave my mother and join his world, the world of men.

The *Elena* drifted at the ledge. We continued with the watches, four hours to a shift, all heads listening for a catch of canvas. But no breeze filled the sails, and a small, inexorable current pushed us toward the drop.

At evening, the hard sun sank below the ledge. With the *Elena* hove to and sideways toward it, the English conscript took a crossbow—he was now inseparable from it—and fired an arrow over. It dropped silently out of view. Alfredo told him he "had missed" and fired another. It too vanished.

At half a league's distance from the ledge, the captain—from his bunk—ordered all the ballast dumped from the ship and the crew to mount the sweeps. We would row the *Elena* back into whatever trades had brought us here. With our barrels of supplies adrift around us, the crew dug the oars in the water the entire night. I laid my quill in the ledger and joined Diego to pull. We sat next to each other on a bench, and in the darkness, he laid his hand atop mine.

Our interpreter, Pinzón, was afraid the motion of the oars

would call the serpents. We set torches along the gunwale, but spotted nothing. Perhaps even the serpents recognized the precipice, the way certain fish know to stop at the mouth of the Guadalquivir and go no further. Despite our hours rowing, the *Elena*'s prow made no progress. The current toward the ledge was too strong.

The captain called out to me. Inside his quarters, he lay dressed in a long, loose tunic, Coralito kneeling at his side. From the hem, Captain Veragua's withered legs stuck out long and rigid as fork tines. He seemed to have lost half his weight.

"How far are we?" he asked. "Coralito cannot see the distance."

"I should think we will meet the ledge in two days' time," I said.

The captain closed his eyes. In the faint light, I made out on his shirt the spottings of blood and grease, where Diego had applied fat as a salve.

"Drop the sea anchors behind us," the captain ordered. "And bring the longboat." He lifted himself up and winced. "Dress me, Coralito," he said.

I did as I was commanded, though his intentions were unclear. I woke Alfredo and Armando to cast the sea anchors. The broad canvas sacks hit the water and swelled. They would slow our drift nearly to a stop, but we would no longer be able to turn and sail. Next, I led the longboat that trailed the *Elena* up amidships. Without sail or mast, the longboat was designed for short islanding journeys. It was a glorified rowboat, shadeless and exhausting. Didn't the captain know we were a thousand leagues from home? Or had his mind fevered past reason?

"You can't row that to Spain," the English conscript said, a slick rat wriggling in his hand. "Not without miracles."

"We're not going back," I said and tied the line of the longboat to a pin.

Pinzón paced the deck, scratching the back of his hand until it bled. "We must be cursed. Some sin lives aboard this ship." He saw me then, his eyes begging me. "Where is the sin, Peralonso?"

The English conscript slit the throat of the rat and held it over the water by the tail as it thrashed and the blood drained into the sea. "Tell him, boy. You know where."

Pinzón looked back and forth, puzzled. A narrow flame coiled inside me, burning away my breath. "My heart is pure," I said.

He brandished his wet knife. The rat went still. "Is that what Diego likes? Your purity?" he said, tongue flickering between his teeth. He hammered his knife into the gunwale and dug his fingers under the flesh as he tore the skin from the body.

The captain tolled the bell. He winced in his officer's trousers, a pouch in his hand, and I fell in with the gathering crew, happy to leave the conscript to his work. "Let us give thanks to God who has thought us worthy to discover such a great wonder, this ledge," the captain began. He shook the pouch. In the sack, he explained, were beans representing the crew of the *Elena*, and among them were four marked with crosses, four

great honors. Each of us would come and take a single bean
and those that pulled a cross would strike out for the ledge.

The men eyed one another. Our captain had admitted that
our great expedition was folly. The countries we knew were
the only countries. But what unimaginable vale awaited us
over the ledge? What did it feel like to fall forever?

The sack was passed from man to man. The English conscript went first, and though I prayed for fortune not to visit
him, he smiled and showed his smooth bean. When Diego
pulled his, he made no expression, which I took for luck. The
carpenter Ginés pulled the first marked one and Pinzón the
second. He rushed to the captain.

"I'm not a seaman, nor have I any skill with a bow," Pinzón
pleaded. "I will be a failure to the crew of that small boat."

The captain rested his charred hand on Pinzón's shoulder.
"Every country, every animal speaks a language. When we
return, you will tell with your best words what you have seen."

"But this plan is death."

The captain said back, "You shall be rewarded. Or face the
lash."

I went last. On the surface of the final bean, I felt the
markings of a knife. The last cross.

The captain asked, "Who is the fourth man?"

I looked to Diego, and he must have seen the fear in me
because he then stepped forward, casting his bean off the side.
He would take my place and leave me alive.

The captain said, "We will leave at dawn."

As the crew scattered across the deck, sinking into their

privacies, I felt a cutting mix of shame and loss. I had been made a coward. The men began to pray for deliverance, for the opportunity to see their fathers and wives and children again, for an everlasting life that I could not understand. I knew only the ache of the present. I thought of my mother pulling a tray of *alfajores* from the oven, scored with the Hebrew letter for righteousness. "The world begins the day we are born," she told me, "and the world will end the day we die."

Under the torchlight, I found Diego on the forecastle, staring out at the drop alone. He looked calm and peaceful and welcomed me with a pat on the deck beside him.

"Why Diego?" I whispered. "Why did you save me?"

His eyes were soft. To my amazement, he took the ledger from my hand and lettered slowly. I had never seen him use a quill. For the first time, I heard his voice.

"YOUNG," he wrote and pointed at my chest. "MORE LIFE."

"But you have life too," I said. "Why are you not afraid?"

He took up his lettering again. "SOMEONE I WISH TO SEE."

A shudder traveled along my spine. Then Diego clutched me, and I felt a finality, as if he were trying to give over whatever part of him I hungered for. He felt solid and strong and then he was gone, crossing the deck to the cook box. Until dawn, he stoked the fires, preparing a breakfast of breads, served with the captain's jars of prunes and jam. I came to him. "Diego," I started, unsure of how to shape into words an ocean of feelings.

He pressed his pinched fingers at my lips. The last time I felt him alive. Powdered cinnamon dusted my mouth and exploded into a rounded, delicious silence.

At dawn, the crew mounted a torch to the prow of the long-boat and cinched the long fathom line to an oarlock. The line would run from the longboat to the *Elena*, to keep it tethered. When the preparations were done, Diego and Ginés lowered the captain into the boat and set him in the bow. In his hand, he held the queen's letters of introduction. At stern, Pinzón pleaded upwards. He'd spent the night writing letters to his wife. At dawn, he burned them all and wrote one to his mistress in Madrid, a letter he sealed with wax and swore me to deliver.

The sun rose as they set out, their oars slapping into a waveless ocean. The hemp line unspooled in lazy jerks. The captain peered out from the bow, his eyes fixed on the approaching ledge. Diego rowed and rowed, never looking up at me though I yearned for some last contact. On the *Elena*, no one spoke as the longboat shrank into the distance. When the second knot on the line passed over the gunwale, Alfredo called out, "Two fathoms gone!"

We never heard their cries. In an instant, the line unwound ferociously and the longboat vanished. The crew jumped on the rope and found themselves nearly propelled over. I grabbed the final length of line and tied it to the base of the main mast. When it uncoiled completely, the rope, three-fingers thick, sprang taut, and the mast groaned. The crew scrambled forward to regain a hold but could not pull the line back. We were strung tight; the fathom line ran from the *Elena*, through the air and over the ledge.

A monstrous pull tilted the ship sidelong and dragged her toward the drop. Everything on deck slid to one side.

Alfredo drew his knife and began to cut the line. But I couldn't let him release Diego and the others to their death. If there is only this life—and nothing after—then it must be defended.

I met him at the rope, his blade already biting in, the line opening like tendon.

"You'll kill them," I said.

"They're lost already," he said. "We'll go with them!"

I wrestled the knife from his hand and tossed it into the sea. Alfredo looked at me as if I were mad. Before I could move, I felt another blade across my throat.

"Cut it," the English conscript called out from behind me.

Armando came to his brother's side and continued the sawing with his own knife. But then my eye caught something out at the ledge: Diego, pulling himself along the rope, hand over hand, back to the *Elena*.

"Look!" Alfredo cried.

Armando stopped. The crew gathered at the line and hove. And this time, the line yielded, and we managed to reclaim it, until it was clear that we were pulling a weight far greater than just Diego. With a final heave, the tension on the line dropped and then we could see the longboat itself crest back through the spume and come to rest on the ocean surface. We had gaffed Diego back onto the deck—he rolled on his back and sank into a stupor—before I noticed the longboat was not empty.

A lone figure sat inside it. A woman.

She sat on one of the benches, in a high-waisted dress with flared sleeves and a heart-shaped hat. She was old and frail and dripping wet. Her skin looked as white as boiled bone.

"Where am I?" she called to us. "I'm frightened."

I knew the *Elena*'s bilge, awash with rotting food and piss, could inspire delusions. Ethers from belowdecks had been known to poison sailors with mirages, even throttle them in sleep. You could be surrounded by fresh sea air and your own ship could suffocate you. But we all saw this woman. Could every man be taken with the same dream?

Coralito peered out, his face blanched. His eyes hunted through his blindness. "Who is there?" he asked.

"A woman," I said. "From beyond the ledge."

"What is your name?" Coralito called out.

The woman swooned. "The sun is burning my skin. I must dry and get out of this heat."

"What is your name!" Coralito called again. "Your name!"

The woman gasped. "Coralito?"

Coralito staggered back and crossed himself. "This cannot be," he said.

"Tell us your name," I called out.

The woman flapped her hat in her face. "My name is Isabela Hernandez Coralito, wife of Fernando Mancuello Coralito."

Coralito hissed, "*She has been dead for six years.*"

The woman cast a glance over her shoulder. "Please," she said. "There are so many others waiting."

We kept her in the longboat. All day the wraith cried out, demanding shade and water. Her voice was so human, so frail and chilling. She tried, fruitlessly, to paddle forward with her hands. When the sun continued to rise in a rinsed sky, she grew more urgent and pained. If she had been alive, truly alive, our treatment—watching an old woman wilt—would have been torture. Instead, as Coralito swore, his wife had passed away. He had set her tombstone himself.

At dusk, Diego gathered strength, though he was now ashen, his skin drained of color. I caved a blanket around him while he stared into the bowl of his hands. They were red and badly cut from his climb back to the boat, one wrist disjointed and swollen where he'd twisted it up in the line. He rehearsed his grip, opening and closing his fingers. I sat beside him, holding the ledger.

"Write," I said. "Tell me. What did you see?"

I noticed, then, his wound: a deep gash at his right wrist that ran through to the other side. Inside, the tissue was gray. Every time Diego rotated his hand, the flesh opened like a mouth and did not bleed. He looked at it queerly.

His letters were feeble and wrong-handed. "DEAD?"

I felt a kick to my leg. "What'd he write?" the English conscript asked, peering on the page. "What're those letters?"

"He's weak," I answered. "We need to leave him alone."

The conscript sized me with cold eyes. "I served ten years for my crime. And you, for yours?"

At the sound of oars in the water, I pushed him off. I stood to see Alfredo and Armando in the fishing dingy. They approached the woman with a small skin of fresh water—their Christian duty—and a crossbow aimed at her chest. Coralito joined them. The dory held still at thirty strokes from the longboat.

"Fernando, why do these men hold their weapons at me?" she called out, nervously.

"Where have you come from?" Coralito asked. "I buried you."

Her hand went to her chest. "What?"

"You died in our bedroom in Aragon, in my arms," Coralito said. "We fell asleep and when I awoke you were gone, Isabela. This was six years ago."

Isabela shook her head. "I don't remember, Fernando. I don't remember any of that."

Armando and Alfredo rowed the dory closer and closer until it knocked the side of the longboat and Coralito stepped over to attend to his wife.

She was fed and given a swath of tarpaulin for shade. While Coralito comforted her, Alfredo and Armando rigged a small shelter with a split-bunk post and cord fixed to the prow. They left Coralito and rowed back to the *Elena*.

"I felt her breath," Armando whispered. "It was cold, like a winter draft."

"Her eyes are black," Alfredo added. "But her pain is as real as any."

By nightfall, Coralito called for the dory. Back on ship, he steadied himself at the mast. "She is no dream," he said.

"What does she know of the captain, of the others?" I asked.

"Where did she come from?" Armando asked.

"It is a peculiar story," Coralito began, chewing his nail. She told him that one day, she awoke on a shoreline crowded with people. The sea there was tideless and still. Inland, trees loomed over the shore, a forest so dense it seemed like a wall. People there wandered along this shore as far as she could see, men and women of many ages, colors, and costumes, speaking in strange tongues. Each appeared to travel alone, and they often stopped her and asked for things, but she was afraid and pulled away. Eventually, she said, she began walking too. She never saw the same face twice.

At one moment, a moment that she could not separate from other moments, Isabela moved into the sea, knee-deep. She had never thought to enter the water before. But something called to her. From the mist, the longboat drifted into her sight. She got in. The crowds from the shore saw and rushed at the water. The fathom line snapped taut and she found herself pulled out to sea. She held tight as a mist enveloped her. The sound of the voices faded until it was replaced by a rumble and the sense of vertiginous turn. The next she knew, she could make out the *Elena*.

Coralito stopped and ran his hand across his face, wiping the disbelief. Armando the Taller crossed himself.

"I asked for her hand and made a cut along her finger,"

Coralito continued. "Her blood is red and real."

"Lie. She doesn't bleed," said the conscript, nodding to Diego. "Just like the mute. They're both wraiths now."

The crew stared at Diego. He did not look up.

I said, "Come morning, we return her to the ledge."

Coralito tugged his tunic taut against his chest. "Then I go with her," he answered. "I will not leave my wife."

"Diego goes too," Armando said.

His brother stepped toward him. "But what if there are others, abandoned over the ledge? Are we to leave them in purgatory?"

Armando shook his head. "Anything else would defy God's will."

Alfredo's face lost its softness. He seemed to rise up his whole length. "You speak of God's will?" he shot back. "Was it God's choice to take our brother? Or yours?"

The brothers leapt on each other and wrestled to the deck. They fought, equally matched, like a man with his reflection. If no one stopped them, it was because we felt we were watching the war within us playing out. Each man aboard—Coralito, the conscript, Diego, Marco, and the other deckhands— understood that the ledge was now among us. We could pass over the edge or we could plunder it, but we could not escape. We watched in silence until the two brothers sat across from each other, exhausted and bruised. Blood ran from Alfredo's nose and his brother rubbed his jaw.

"I remember him," Alfredo said. "He was our brother. And if he is still alive, I will go and get him myself."

That night, there was no reversing of the sand clock, no order to the *Elena*. Coralito boarded the dory and was rowed out to his wife. The men drained the wine casks and fired all the supplies in a noisy feast. Diego stood at the prow, ignoring me, even more pale, like alabaster. He paced, the way a wife grooves a path of anticipation on a widow's walk, and stared out at the ledge. I could find no consolation in the riot around me and the chill air had me missing the simple heat of my mother's bakery. Why had I ever left? Why is it that men are always leaving? What is this hunger for what we can't see? I ached for the Calle de la Mar, for the sounds of the fruit carts jostling, and to see one more time my mother at the doorway and to smell her honey cakes rolling out into the street. I called to her in a prayer. I wanted to see her face again and feel blessed, but I could not summon the whole of it. It remained blurred, like smoked glass, and the knowledge that I had forgotten it filled me with a clawing emptiness. The night wore on. The crew's exuberance faded into melancholy, and they keened for their families and home cities, for those they would never see again. I fell asleep in a curl of loose sail.

I woke to a jerk. Under the first kindling of clouds, the fathom line was already strung out to the ledge and Alfredo, Diego, and others, with a great cry, pulled together.

"What are you doing?" I asked. None turned to answer me.

Armando shoved his way forward, shouting, "This is blasphemy!" But before he could fight, the longboat returned over the ledge and came through the spray, laden with three new figures.

"Armando? Alfredo?" yelled a young man, standing in the boat. "Is that you? I felt you calling me!"

Armando stepped toward the gunwale, squinting, his mouth open.

"Brother!" Alfredo called back. "We're both here! Come to us!"

The longboat knocked alongside the *Elena*, and Alfredo lifted the young man to the deck with a stevedore's strength. He looked just like the brothers, though youngest, and his skin had no pigment. He hugged Alfredo with genuine pleasure.

"You seem so old," he said. "Have you been away?"

"No, no," his brother said beaming. "It's *you* who left *us*."

Armando made the sign of the cross. "You are dead," he said. "I took your life."

A laugh shot out of his brother. "You took nothing."

A boy followed up the rope ladder, unkempt, in tattered trousers. He was not more than five or six years old, and a swollen lump rested at the base of his neck. It had been years since I'd seen a mark of the plague. The boy stood bewildered by the unfamiliar faces until the ship's gimbaling startled him and he began to shake and cry. Diego pushed his way forward to face the child.

"My son," he said, collapsing around the boy. "My son."

Diego's voice. The sound of it shattered me, the deepest chime of the closest, celestial sphere.

When the final figure boarded the *Elena*, holding her head

down in humility, I knew that I had called her. Those who crossed the ledge did so because we summoned them with yearning. Her shirt was soaked, a damp rag giving no warmth, though none was needed. When she looked up, I understood why the crew had mutinied: Death is the tyranny. To conquer the ledge was a conquest over this. The greed of time.

My mother stood before me, wet and shivering in her resurrection. Her black eyes studied me in a bloodless face.

I embraced her, and as I did, I noticed the odd twist in her body, her neck stretched. An angry, red indentation wrapped around her throat. My fingers sought it out and ran these ridges where rope had once been.

"I told you to never leave," my mother said.

My strength left and I buried myself in her hair. "Forgive me," I said. I remained there until I felt a lock of it brush against my face in a breeze.

From where I sit, I watch the crew busy with lines. Every one is now strung over the ledge. In time, each snaps taut and the deckhands pull first the longboat, then a handful of crude rafts around the ledge, heavy with people. Soon, the *Elena* is crowded with men and women, in all kinds of dress and colors, my mother among them. I write in the ledger, "Many new souls."

By afternoon, the crew sends the longboat one last time over the drop. This time, they cut free the sea anchors and raise the mainsail for a broad reach. A westerly favors us, and even before our sails are half-raised, the *Elena* heaves forward with life. An enormous weight drags on us and hemp lines split, some tear from their braces.

Finally a Portuguese galleon crests through the spume, with dozens of people clutching to its deck. The *Elena* has towed it over. The white faces look as if they have survived a squall, as if they are amazed to be alive. Eventually the men of the galleon set its sails and drop more lines back into the roar.

They pull over a strange ship, this one low and open and driven by oars, with a high wooden dragonhead fixed at its prow. The two ships repeat this, and before long, the sea here becomes busy with boats, many unknown to me, and far outnumbering the *Elena*. The water carries the noise of weird cries. This motley army of the dispossessed, recovered from the ledge, soon fills the ocean as far as I see. At evening, we depart east together, toward home, sails bellied in the new wind.

Everything, All at Once

My mother calls. "I have lichen," she says. "On my vagina."

What can be done? I am her daughter. I accept.

"Lichen is a woods thing," I answer. "A hiking thing."

My mother lives on the tenth floor of a high-rise that over-looks New York Harbor from a New Jersey bluff. She leaves only to shop, to return half of what she has bought, and to eat lunch at the Quick Check. She has not been hiking or on lichen or lichen-adjacent since before I knew what a vagina was. Her adventures are happy hours in the penthouse bar, where she counts the freighters and container ships in the harbor with Al, a retired sea captain.

"Well, the Internet says I have it inside me," she says, "and you can't tell a soul."

It is Saturday morning. I open my garage door, the phone compacted between my ear and shoulder. Inside, the mau-soleum of my marriage—the shelves and stacks and piles—greets me with a grim exhale. The papers arrived from the lawyer yesterday. Soon I will be officially divorced from Scott. I'm selling what I can.

"You have to come with me to the doctor," my mother says.

Except I have buyers coming. I'm expecting to get money for my past life. The pleasure of seeing things go.

"This is your mother speaking," she says. "This is your mother in need."

What can ever be done?

I say, "Give me an hour."

At noon a girl drives up in a pickup with her Mexican boyfriend. They saw my ad on Craigslist and are trying to outfit their life in a day. Already they look numb, zombified by exertion. She sucks the final drops from a Gallon Guzzler, pegging the ice with the straw for more. Her boyfriend wears a sweat-soaked, red and yellow T-shirt that reads "YALE." I don't think those are the colors, but things get random on the boardwalk. He massages her shoulders when she stands still. He is shorter and has to reach up a little. In the bed of the truck, a mint green refrigerator is lashed down haphazardly with straps, like an escape trick nobody wants to see.

"How come you want to get rid of so much awesomeness?" the girl asks, her fingers tracing the scalloped rim of a Waterford crystal bowl: a wedding gift that I used for loose change. Her boyfriend picks through a basket of shells and conches, carefully spaced and layered with towels, that I displayed in a glass cabinet at our old place. We lived a hundred yards from the shore, yet I thought we needed reminding about the ocean. My whole marriage felt like that, a reminder that the real thing was close and available but out of view.

"I left my husband four months ago," I say. "All this reminds me of him. Of us."

The girl glances over at her boyfriend. "Don't tell him that," she says, under her breath. "He's wicked superstitious."

I see their relationship unscroll in front of me—his fears, her fears of his fears, the double braid of accommodation and resentment—I want to tell her: *Run*. The divorced aren't jaded. We're clairvoyant.

The boyfriend presses two conches against his ears and grins. I say, "I give that basket to you. No money. *Mi casa, tu casa.*"

"He's not retarded," the girl says.

The boyfriend looks surprised, then honored, then seems to see the basket for what it is, which is a wicker container of beach trash, another weight he'll have to carry. He deposits the conches and turns to a shelf of puzzles. I had a jigsaw period.

They leave with the crystal bowl, coffeemaker, nightstand, single mattress, artificial Christmas tree, and miter saw. Without asking, I carry the basket of shells to their truck. I smell the creamy coconut of suntan lotion and a funky undertone, brackish and tidal. Shards of sanded beach glass rumble like fogged irises inside a cookie tin. Scott and I lived at the beach for five years, and if you could watch just our beach episodes, we would look happy. Scott would fish in the surf or play his guitar, and I would read or just listen, jealous of his aptitudes. I'm a librarian at the elementary school; what I'm good at is cataloging. After every good time we had, I had an assignment for myself. I had to take one shell home, something singular. Proof that I'd felt loved, that I was experiencing what there was to experience. That display case was my own library, a library of moments.

I set the basket down in the truck bed and wonder what the girl will make of it. Will she see the bounty of the Jersey coast, or just me, a forty-one-year-old woman, alone and childless, her diseased mother for a best friend? I am her future. I want to tell her that after their marriage ends—after he cheats, or spends his days stoned, or gambling, or gets up from the table when she asks him for a child—she should pass the shells right on down to the next girl. Souvenirs from what happens later.

She peels the money from a roll as thick as her fist. "We don't want your basket," she says.

"Good," I say, taking it back. "Because I don't like your look."

Dr. Stecopoulos is Greek, in his midthirties, and my mother adores him. Every time we've met, he seems as if he's just come from an exam that he knows he's aced. He patiently allows my mother to pry into his parents' immigration, his years of school, his new marriage. After every detail, my mother throws a look in my direction: *Thessaloníki! Isn't Thessaloníki wonderful?* He is my mother's ideal man at a time when her interactions have become transactional. He has warm hands, walks her to the reception desk. He wears patent leather Italian shoes ("He doesn't skimp," my mother said), and tolerates her jokes, the signal flares of her personality.

She has her legs up in the stirrups, holding her breath, with her hands crossed over her belly. Dr. Stecopoulos probes indistinctly under the paper gown while I perch on a stool by his desk. A bluish plastic model of a uterus rests next to the computer monitor, and it looks drained and baleful, as if it doesn't belong in the light. A little door is open in the front, a dollhouse entrance. What's inside? A pink secret. I could crawl in and rest.

"Well, you were right," the doctor says. "This is definitely lichen sclerosis." He pokes his head up from under the gown. "Do you want to take a look?"

"Ah, no thank you," I say.

"He wasn't talking to you," my mother says. He positions a mirror for her to see. I don't want to look, not even by accident. My phone says I have a message from Scott. He got the papers too. The end is here, and I'm sure he wants to talk. I fiddle with the uterus model. The tiny door in front will not close properly, and I want it closed, in place.

"Have you been sexually active?" Dr. Stecopoulos asks.

"No," I say. "She definitely has not."

My mother remains quiet, staring up at the ceiling.

"Edith?" the doctor asks.

"Mom?" I ask.

She closes her eyes and sighs. "Yes," she says.

The tiny door snaps off in my hand. "What? With who?" I ask.

"I don't need to know that information," Dr. Stecopoulos says. "But you will need to tell all your sexual partners." He delivers this line as if it were plausible that my mother had a sexual partner. My mother is seventy-one. She is in menopause; there is no menoplay. Then he tells her she'll need to apply a steroid cream to her labia—I see the zincky, frosted lips of skiers—and he writes her a prescription.

"With these steroids," my mother asks, dressing, "will my labia become stronger?"

"Gross," I say, and hand Dr. Stecopoulos the door to the uterus. It looks like the piece that covers a battery compartment on a remote, the part that inevitably breaks. "I think I messed up your model."

Dr. Stecopoulos has no idea what I'm talking about.

"Your uterus," I say. "I broke it."

"Oh, that's all right," he says. "My uterus broke a long time ago."

My mother pats his hand. "You're not missing anything."

In the car, my mother hunts desperately in her purse for Coffee Nips, as though she were the person I remember her being. "I need your support right now," she says.

"Fine," I say. "But I'm allowed to say, 'Ew.'"

She closes her eyes, leans back against the headrest, and sucks on her candy with deep delight. She's wearing the clip-on sunglasses I bought for her and a white sport fleece, collar up. I notice now that she got dressed up for the doctor visit in gold, drapey pants and sapphire blouse from *Shine Daughters!*—a fashion catalog she loves, even though it's for African American women—on the off chance that Dr. Stecopoulos would run away with her. The poignancy of my mother's life is that she still thinks people are looking at her, for guidance, for fashion tips. On her bureau, she keeps a framed photo of herself as a teenager in the Atlantic City parade: a red-haired mermaid on a papier-mâché splash, gazing upon the crowd with a royal look. When I was a girl, after she divorced my father and went feminist and vegetarian—Oh my God, the lentils, the antinuke walkabouts, the woven totes of my youth—I used to stare at that photo and wish for it to come alive, for her to invite me up onto the float. I ached to be her so badly I made her bookmarks with declarations of love. As a girl, I would watch her leave to go jogging, braless and single and alive, and wait patiently with her pack of cigarettes for when she returned.

Now she uses a cane, tucked next to her in the passenger seat; she's used it irregularly since her foot surgery, and I know it humiliates her. Men seem almost regal with canes. But women are expected to keep their balance forever. Dime-sized freckles blot her skin, the star chart of her body gaining constellations yearly. A youth spent at the shore is catching up with my mother.

She smiles. This doctor visit has given her a sense of drama, an urgency that cuts a path through the hours. Other times, she can spend a day moving bills around.

"What are you looking at?" she asks.

"I'm trying to see you how your lover sees you," I say.

"Oh, please." She scratches at the corner of her mouth. "I'm starving, and I need my prescription."

"I have to get home," I say. "I have more people coming."

"Good," she says. "There's a Quick Check near you."

When my mother married my father, she was a good Catholic girl, a virgin. "Mistake number one," she told me once. "I hadn't even been down there yet." She divorced my father thirty years ago, and somewhere in her apartment is a photoalbum of all her boyfriends since: Val, the therapist; Devon, my elementary school teacher; and the ape with sideburns who worked in the anthropology department at the college. As we drive, I'm bothered, I realize, by the thought that someone finds my mother attractive. I feel excluded.

"It's Al, isn't it?" I say. Al, the retired ship's captain, who wears blue khakis and a little anchor pin on his cardigan. Al, who plies her with highballs and Manhattans at dusk. He has furry Popeye forearms and a dimly lit Pacific backstory. I picture him on top of my mother, gritting his teeth and thrusting upward, like a ship cresting a wave.

"Wasn't it funny how you broke the uterus?" my mother says.

"Just tell me if it's Al," I say.

She adjusts an air vent. "You should know that he is very gentle," she says. "And appreciative. He understands a woman's body."

I shiver. My mother can't bend over and instead has to spread her legs and squat. Her skin itches constantly, a side effect of her Parkinson's medication. She keeps a back scratcher in her car and another, the telescoping kind, in her purse for emergencies. She can eat a half gallon of ice cream for dinner. People like her should not be having sex; sex is the reward for *not* eating a half gallon of ice cream.

"What's your problem?" she says. "You want so badly to judge me."

"I'm just surprised," I say. "Surprised and worried about you."

She gazes out the window as if she hasn't heard me. "It's not too late for you," she says. "You've been separated from Scott for long enough. It's time to meet new people."

"I'm not ready."

"What about that one I showed you?" she says. "The guy from the Internet?" She has taken to trolling the Craigslist personals for me, trying to matchmake. She'll call and read me the postings: "He says he'll be at the Harborside having a drink for the next hour. I'll go by and check him out for you." *No!* Or: "This one says he likes Bruce Springsteen." *We live in New Jersey; that's redundant!* She is unable to understand that Craigslist is where people sell their junk, including their personalities. No genuine, non-pot-smoking, non-gambling, non-fucking-a-twenty-five-year-old-teacher's-aide-at-your-school man will let the universe know he's having a drink at the Harborside. It's an SOS from the bottom of the dating pool.

"There is no 'guy from the Internet,' and there will never be," I say, my pronouncement punctuated by the speed bump at the entrance to my parking lot. Outside my garage, a man leans against the trunk of a Mercedes convertible. His legs are crossed, and while he talks on his cell phone, he digs at his molars with a pinkie. He's dressed in the Manhattan palette:

charcoal pants, a black short-sleeve dress shirt, and ribbony sandals that make his feet look bloodless. No wedding ring. I park and he finishes his call. "What about him?" my mother whispers as I bound out to meet him.

"You're fifteen minutes late," he says. "I thought you were going to be a no-show."

"I'm sorry. My mother had a doctor's appointment."

"That's me!" My mother waves the palm of the back scratcher from the passenger seat.

"I'm just here for the baby shit," he says.

I throw open the garage door and point. The "baby shit" is in the back, where I could throw a blanket over it and pretend it was a mountain in the distance. I have a bassinet, baby chair, stroller, and play "environment." When Scott and I were trying for kids, I made the mistake of accepting all of this from friends who had had their children, who were done having them. But I never got pregnant. Scott refused to get a fertility test because it was "annoying," then "expensive," then finally "against his religion," the religion of morning bong loads, apparently. My fallopian tubes weren't cooperating either; maybe they knew better. When I moved out, I wasn't quite ready to see it all go, not because I hadn't given up on kids—I'm fine, don't pity me. My first night in the apartment, my mattress pinched at the back of the moving van, I laid out the play environment and fell asleep in it. I slept historically well.

He pulls back the blanket as if uncovering a body in a morgue. "How much for everything?" He is driving a fifty-thousand-dollar car and buying thirdhand baby furniture. I don't press.

"I'll take seventy-five," I say.

"Done," he says. On his way out with the stroller, he picks up the biggest shell in the basket. It's a fan the size of a dinner plate and bleach white. "You giving these away?" he says.

I found that shell one night when Scott and I were fooling around under a pier. I had taken a black-and-white photography class—I wanted a hobby, it seemed validating—and we'd gone there to fill out my portfolio. Scott was high and determined to go down on me, but first I made him pose. Afterwards, I plucked the shell from the sand, an amateur naturalist. The photographs, though, were bad, dark, and indistinct.

"Sorry," I say. "Keepsake." Before, I was eager to give the shells away. But now I don't want this man to have them.

He picks up a mottled brown and pink conch, flawless. "What about this one?" he asks, and I'm back in the tide, our first summer together, bonfire on the beach. "Look what I found," I said to Scott, and he pulled me to him. "Look what *I* found," he whispered, and squeezed my hips.

I don't want these memories.

"Look, you can find all these shells on the beach," I say.

"I don't have time for the beach," says the man with the convertible.

I won't relent, and he shrugs. I help him with the stroller. It fits sideways, recklessly, in his passenger seat, ready to launch.

"It seems like you're shedding," he says.

"Shedding?" I say, irritated.

"You should call me," he says. "I'm a therapist. I see things." He jabs a business card out between two fingers.

I tell him I'm good, and he answers, "Suit yourself."

My mother remains in the passenger seat, a heap of Coffee Nip wrappers in her lap. "He seemed like a hot prospect," she says, his car revving out into the street.

"He just bought baby stuff off Craigslist," I say. "Not a prospect."

"Well, *you* sold it there," she says.

My phone has four messages: two cancellations and two from Scott.

My mother and I buy burritos at the Quick Check and pick up her prescription at Walgreens, but the fact of the two items, the vaginal steroid and our food now in the same bag, erases my appetite. On her balcony, with its sweeping view of the parking lot, I watch her chew her carefully managed bites. My mother has one brave molar left. A heavy breeze brushes the plants and lifts our napkins.

"You need to call Al," I say, fetching the phone. "He could be a vector."

"You love me vulnerable," she says. "It makes you feel whole."

"I'm being cautious," I say. "I'm being *you*." How true and how awful that is. There must be a place in between parent and child, a way to take care of each other without resentment and hating yourself.

"Well, stop," she says, and stands unsteadily. "Don't be me.

Nobody should be me." She walks inside without her cane, lurching from one piece of furniture to another. One of the sad aspects of getting older, I think, is that you lose control over the quality of your entrances and exits. She sits on the couch, in the dark, and I hear her dial and leave a message for Al. A small happiness, the satisfaction of someone following instructions, rises in me.

"What happened?" I call to her.

"Leave me alone."

"What? He's not there?"

"He does his power walking on Saturdays," she says. "Why don't you go upstairs to happy hour, to the bar?" She wants to shower and apply her salve in private. I'm happy to leave and take the good magazines with me.

When the elevator door opens into the Penthouse Lounge, I feel as if I'm stepping onto the pleasure deck of a 1970s cruise ship, all aquamarine and pink extravagance, smelling vaguely of pizza dough and shrimp cocktail, the aroma of recent fun. I pull a chair to the floor-to-ceiling window. At this hour, the building's shadow stretches way out into the Atlantic. Scott and I came up here just once, right after my mother moved in, and he pointed out the whole sweep, from the Palisades to the knobby tip of Long Island. He knew the geography. Below, Sandy Hook arcs out toward Manhattan. The people on it are just dots of color; maybe one is collecting shells, trying to hold the afternoon still. I could call Scott.

I should call Scott.

Living at the beach was his idea. I'd thought of other places for us—Philadelphia, Hoboken—but he wanted to sit at the beach in the sun and think and "see what surfaced." Here I am, at the top floor, doing it without him. What we take from each other, without knowing. I remember Sundays, he'd prop his fishing pole up in the sand, park himself in a lawn chair, and stare out at the water, watching night come. Once, near the end, I showed him a perfect nautilus I'd found. He palmed it. "This used to be something's *house*," he said with an emphasis that told me he was high, long after he'd promised to stop. "A house, until something died." And I saw the curl of emptiness inside the shell and it was all I could see. All that armor protecting a darkness, really, an ending.

The elevator dings, and old men in baseball caps and windbreakers spill out. They discover me alone at the window and give me a wide berth. I'm probably some fantasy they've all had: the teary girl in the penthouse bar. They begin stretching on the floor, their legs up on tables, flexing. Not one has broken a sweat. It's impossible to tell if they're about to leave or are finishing up. I recognize Al in a yellow tracksuit and spotless white sneakers. His headphone-radio, a novelty of twenty years ago, loops around his neck. He smiles, and all I can see is complicated dentistry.

"You need to talk to my mother," I say to him.

He looks concerned, almost as if he cared. "What's the matter?"

"She'll tell you about it."

"Is she hurt?"

"She's . . . coping," I say, righteous and inviolable. I am her daughter. I have her interests at heart.

"I'll do that," he says with chronic gentlemanliness. I smell a peppery gust of aftershave, cologne, and sweat. When he asks if I'm all right, I huff at him. He backs away, giving me my space, except now I don't want it.

"Look, I just want you to take responsibility for your actions," I call out. He's bent over now, fingers about three feet from touching his toes. Al cranes himself out of position, his hands on his lower back, and comes back.

"Do you love her?" I ask. His eyebrows furrow.

"Your mother and I are good friends."

"Friends with benefits?"

"Benefits?" he says, confused. "Like life insurance?"

The other men whisper to each other. The words boil out of me. "Oh, don't play dumb. What is this place? Some kind of sex castle?" The others step toward the elevator. I know I look insane, but I'm right. If I'm not having sex, they're not allowed to either.

Al sighs. "Your mother told me about you, what you're going through."

Of course she told him. She used me to get him. Because that's what mothers do: they get us to run errands with them, wait patiently with cigarettes, take notes at the doctor's. And then use our sadness as a story, as a friendship appetizer.

"You know something?" I say. "You've ruined her."

Al shakes his head. "Grow up, sweetheart. Your pain's driving this car."

Which makes no sense! I grip the magazines into a tight coil and shake them at his nose like a dog. "Love is driving this car, asshole!"

Al squints and cocks his head. "I think we're talking about different vehicles."

I flee down the emergency stairs like a grown-up, humiliated, in flight from myself.

Back in her apartment, my mother naps on the couch in her bathrobe, with two cucumber slices over her eyes. She looks like a surprised cartoon character. And in her expression, in the small truth of vegetable matter on her face, I see that my mother has not given up. She is not done, not over, and I must make allowances. I kneel next to her and take her hand.

"Shhh," she says. "The cream is doing its magic. It's tingly."

"I need to leave," I say. "I need to be alone."

She kisses my hand. "Go do you."

I call Scott from the beach, the empty shell basket at my feet, in the surf.

"Thank God you called, baby," he says. "I'm falling apart here."

"Remember those shells," I say, "the ones from that cabinet?"

"No," he says. "Not really."

"Wait," he says. "Maybe. Yeah."

A wave comes, splashes up to my knee. I feel the last shell brush against my leg as it goes. "The tide just came and took them," I tell him. "Everything, all at once."

Hazard 9

1.

From the passenger bench of the Origin Resources surveying helicopter, Leland Barr gripped his shoulder belt and leaned over to take in the end of King Mountain. The summit, jutting out of the dissipating fog, looked like a kneecap rising out of a bath. Bright yellow company dozers worked the shale along a series of plateaus and ramps. Draglines pulled spoil rock down the south face. Typically, nothing made Leland feel more executive, more ascendant, than the unmaking of a ridge. Nature always gave, under the fuse. But today, he felt blunted, elsewhere. Merrill had taken the dog.

The chopper eased up over the ridge, and a patch of undisturbed grass came into view, at the far end of the summit. "What's that?" Leland asked into the headset.

The pilot veered and Leland saw rows of granite and marble stones. At center was a one-room shack with a corrugated tin roof, caked in moss. At the perimeter, an oak tree lay poled out on the ground, root ball lofted in the air.

"Graveyard," the pilot answered. "Turned up during the raze."

Nearby, Origin boys in hardhats mixed with some motley group, trespassers probably, and Leland wearily understood that somebody had an opinion he didn't want to hear. Already, he wanted a drink, his flask tucked into the ruffled pocket of his briefcase.

Six months ago, when Origin first opened King for extraction, Leland's picture ran on the front page of the Louisville paper. Sometime that night, "MOUNTAIN JUSTICE LEAGUE," was splashed in red paint on his garage in Indian Hills. A pile of tree stumps materialized in his drive, deposited by huffy females and snaggletoothed young men who wanted the country to plug into the Persian Gulf, apparently. As the mountain came down, the vandalism escalated—dozer tires slashed during a site visit, his face with fangs stapled to telephone poles along Frankfort Avenue, the driveway gate padlocked shut . . . Corporate paid for the cleanup, but the antagonism had taken its toll. Merrill told him she didn't "want to live in a bull's-eye." She worked for a cancer nonprofit that ushered more pink into the world. She felt above enemies. In the spring, they'd separated and she'd taken an apartment near Cherokee Park, and just this weekend, she'd come back for the terrier. "Something's broke in you, Leland," she said on the stoop, Murphy struggling in her arms. "And I don't think you know what it is yet."

The pilot set down the helicopter on the plateau near the site office, a row of connected trailers on cinder blocks. Leland grabbed his briefcase, ducked out into the gust of the blades, and the heat hit him. The sun had a rare intensity on shadeless ground—site visits felt like a pit stop on a hot plate. Out from the downdraft, he donned sunglasses and cuffed his sleeves. He would go through the motions of being himself. The soil was cracked and hard-packed underneath him, but small weeds still sprung up. There was always life after a leveling. The site manager waved to him urgently at the open door of the office. The blades of the chopper slowed and Leland heard the rattle of generators, the beeps of the dozers and loaders across the site, and, in the distance, the shouting.

2.

Kyle watched Squirrel from the far end of the chain of people, glad to be at maximum distance from the conflict. His stomach pitched and rolled, unhappy with the maybe-not-entirely-cooked tofu scramble Squirrel had made for the action team at dawn. A delirium had set in, and it occurred to Kyle that vomiting was not out of the question.

"There is supposed to be a fifty-foot green perimeter around this!" Squirrel yelled, pulling the chain of people forward. "How many times do we need to say it? That is the *law*!" Squirrel's face was flush and blotchy, his hair tucked under his "lucky" blue bandana and his beard gone pubic, giving him a mutinous zeal. Kyle had wanted to bring baseball caps, something for shade, but Squirrel nixed them. He looked over Kyle's collection—like the one that had a unicorn and "Meet Me at the Creation Museum!" on it—and pronounced them "off message." "There might be media," Squirrel explained solemnly, which Kyle knew meant a person with a cell phone and laser-printed media badge. Kyle was still learning to get "on message," still deciding if he liked it.

Kyle watched Squirrel's boots sink into the cracked earth in front of the bulldozer and wondered how much longer any of this had to last. The fight, this action, his relationship to Squirrel, all in the mix of the nausea. The older woman next to Kyle, wearing an oversized T-shirt with a picture of her cat on it, vice-gripped his hand. It was the only thing keeping Kyle upright.

"Which part of private property don't you dipshits get?" yelled back one of the miners in an orange vest. His hand rested on the wheel hub of a bulldozer. "This is a *fucking* work zone. It's not safe."

An argument in the full-bore sun, miles from Squirrel's truck and cell signal, and hours from the city, was the opposite of safe. Squirrel had asked Kyle to come join the action, to be "a witness for the mountain," which Kyle had assumed meant s'mores and maybe a tent-bound blowjob. But there were no tents. There was no camping. There was, however, much yelling. He'd been dragged here, and now he had a low-grade dysentery for the cause.

Kyle wasn't political. He'd moved to Louisville to work as a designer for the alt-weekly, which promptly went out of business, and in the spiral of his funemployment, he fled his apartment and took long walks along Bardstown Road. He'd seen Squirrel inside the Justice League storefront, leaning almost horizontal in a chair, wearing a knit vest and that blue bandana and smoking a corncob pipe, like you could just do that and not look ridiculous. It was the case that Kyle had always had a thing, unspoken and alarming in its power, for the guy on the Brawny paper towels. Kyle went inside and asked for "some literature," trying to seem both curious and manly with indifference. The pink triangle on Squirrel's squalid messenger bag was all the proof he needed.

"You want to know about the corporate skull-fuck of the planet?" Squirrel said, and pointed to a television, where footage of landslides ran in a loop. Mud slurry paved its way down mountain slopes. "How much literature can you handle?"

Squirrel was, as it turned out, the literature. At the start, Kyle loved listening to him, the long filigreed monologues of invective, the precision of his authority. Undoubtedly, Kyle had enjoyed the minor and probably imaginary cachet of sleeping with a bisexual local activist who played the mandolin and read constantly, whose immodest, uncut penis Kyle considered, privately, the only virgin hardwood worth caring about. Squirrel's behaviors—shitting with the bathroom door open, eating a single spoonful of sugar for dessert—fascinated Kyle zoologically. But dating Squirrel, a boy *named* Daniel who *answered* to Squirrel, was like sleeping with a stray. Squirrel would disappear for action weekends and return with a pinecone. The fact that the dollar store didn't have vegetarian black beans might set him off. He carried with him a caustic tea-tree extract that he used to bathe *and* wash dishes. It was awful to think, but maybe the nausea gave Kyle a certain clarity: he had to break it off before it turned bad, before Squirrel decided girls were where it was at or went off to sleep in the woods.

"What part of cemetery don't you get? These are *graves*," shouted another activist, followed by a chorus of agreement. Kyle's stomach foamed again. The older woman next to him looked over skeptically. She lived in the hollow at the base of the mountain, in a ramshackle house with a washing machine full of green water out on the front lawn. That morning, she had led the group up the mountain, intuitively moving through the woods like Leatherstocking in blown-out Velcro sneakers. They'd passed a sign tacked to a tree, "DANGER BLASTING." She'd given it the finger.

"Young man, you're tilting, you know that?" she said. "Do you need to sit?"

Her hand was tough and dirty and Kyle was working at not thinking about that, because thinking about it seemed to lift his breakfast up and out. Puking would definitely be off-message. "I'm fine," Kyle said.

A miner lifted himself into the cabin of the dozer and the engine chugged to life. Black smoke belched from the exhaust. Squirrel stepped up and onto the blade, in full revolutionary mode. Kyle had seen this before, when Squirrel straightened his back and startled people with his ardor.

"Until the site ceases being in violation," Squirrel declared, "we will *not* be going anywhere."

Up the ridge, two men, one in a dress shirt and carrying a briefcase, made their way down. A negotiator, Kyle hoped, since he, personally, was not planning on wilting much longer. Even if it meant bushwhacking by himself back down to Squirrel's pickup somewhere down the mountain.

The foreman spat a slug of tobacco at Squirrel's feet and nodded to the driver up in the dozer. "I don't get paid enough for this bullshit."

The next few seconds Kyle saw in a kind of glare, an admixture of heatstroke and mild arousal at his boyfriend's leadership skills. The dozer jumped when it went into gear and Squirrel's ankle failed. He slipped, hands wheeling, and the side of his head slammed into the edge of the metal blade. His body crumbled as though someone had cut his strings. The crowd gasped and Kyle bent over and yawned up breakfast, the last thing Squirrel would ever give him.

3.

Leland turned off the television in the sunroom and let the whir of the crickets fill the house. All the windows open with the central air gusting: his preferred climate. Outside, the line of plants, a hydrangea and magnolia and something Merrill had mocked him for not knowing, brushed against the screens in the evening breeze. From the recliner, he could see out to the backyard, the grass gone to seed, the gazebo where they'd had drinks in its dappled shadows all of once, when, for a moment, they took renewed pleasure in each other's company. Now, the lattice and structure was buried under the growth, a trophy some vine had claimed.

Since Merrill's departure, the sunroom had become the whole house for Leland—office, bar, bed, kitchen, throne. A hole he'd fallen into. Evenings, he worked from here, whiskey on the TV-dinner stand, next to the corporate laptop. Murphy's empty dog bowl remained at the base of the cabinet, where a population of liquor bottles awaited their god, the maid.

Leland was letting things go. He was seeing where they went.

He rose and dumped a half-eaten carton of Chinese into the sink. There, on the countertop, next to his computer, was the boy's blue bandana, folded into a square. The maid had washed the blood out. He picked it up and noticed lettering in the material, barely legible, made with a ballpoint pen: "The end of every civilization begins with the end of the trees."

The evacuation had been Leland's decision. The haul roads down were too rough, the trail too uneven and long, to carry the boy out. So they got him on a stretcher and back up to the Origin chopper while he fell in and out of consciousness. Leland got in, followed by another young man—the boy's friend or handler, with some kind of ill-advised moustache. Later, he would discover that his briefcase had gone missing in the chaos and wonder, acidly, if the awfulness had been staged. On the ride, the young man with the moustache gripped his friend's limp hand. The gesture was careful and tender, and Leland found himself staring. Homosexuals, albeit unkempt ones. The pilot raised University Hospital on the radio, and the moment they landed, emergency medics whisked the body inside. But the young man remained on the chopper bench, uncertain.

"What do I do?" he asked.

The question surprised him. Leland answered, "You go look after him. That's what you do."

It was only later, back at Bowman Field, that Leland discovered he still had the bandana in his hand. And the awful moment returned: the boy, looking up at Leland with astonishment and single bloodshot eye before he drifted. A week later, the boy remained at the hospital with a skull fracture. Of course, without insurance. Origin would cover the substantial costs. The newspapers had not yet bit on the story, and certainly would neglect to mention the corporate beneficence.

The doorbell rang. Leland wondered if he'd ordered food twice and forgotten. Under the porch light, the young man from the helicopter, the handler with the eyebrow along his top lip, dawdled on his front step. His face seemed sharper, less comedic, and he wore a T-shirt emblazoned with a squidlike monster throttling the city skyline. Below it ran the words "Release the Kraken!" In his hand, he had Leland's briefcase.

"I think this is yours," the young man said.

Steadying himself on the doorframe, Leland accepted it with what he hoped was unbleary firmness. The weight seemed correct, though the flask would certainly be missing. There'd been nothing of consequence inside: everything that mattered was on his laptop.

"I assume it's been thoroughly pawed?" Leland said.

The young man shrugged. "I don't know. I'm not part of them. You should have it. It's yours."

"How's your friend?" Leland asked.

"Still in the hospital. There's swelling. On his brain."

"All right then." But the moment hung between them. The boy's face summoned up the last time they'd been together, on the roof of the hospital, when he looked to Leland with needfulness. He and Merrill had never had children— the treatments had impeded her fertility—but with the young man now in front of him he felt an odd calling. The night suddenly seemed to require a charity that Leland could just about deliver.

"Have a nice life," the young man said, and turned to walk up the drive.

Later, Leland would understand it had been a mistake to allow the boy this close, to permit him to study his privacy, but the months of drinking had sanded down his discernment. And he'd come all this way, miles into the county, simply to return what was his.

"Hang on just one a moment, son," Leland said. "What do you drink?"

4.

Kyle sat bolt upright in the lawn chair, as though he might be graded. The interior of the gazebo was a green cave—lights strung up along the lattice made him feel like they'd crawled inside the private heart of the plant. Barr had hacked their way inside, tearing at the vine, wrestling with something prior and clearly still present. Kyle hesitated before he followed. The guy was half off his face, marinating in alcohol, and curious about all the wrong things. Did serial killers like plants?

"And just what is a 'kraken'?" Leland Barr asked. "And why do you want it released?"

"The kraken is a monster," Kyle said. "It's supposed to be funny."

Kyle sipped his drink tentatively—Barr had made them both bourbon and coke with "two jiggers" of liquor—and checked the time on his phone. He felt trapped, though Barr was harmless.

"Well, I'm not a monster," Barr said. "Whatever your friends say."

"They're not my friends," Kyle said.

"And the hospital? Are they taking care of him?" Barr drained his drink.

"I don't know. His mother doesn't want me there."

Squirrel's mother had, in fact, hated him instantly. She lashed at him, as though he were to blame, and yet he was—by anyone's measure—the furthest from it. "Stay away from my son," she'd said in the hospital parking lot where he'd gone to greet her, and then promptly barred him from the room where Squirrel lay prone and silent. None of the Mountain Justice League had sided with him, the gay boyfriend, the outlier. Instead, they drew a perimeter of care around Squirrel that didn't include him, didn't include *that* kind of justice. When

she turned away, he saw the patch for a horse farm emblazoned across the back of her denim jacket. It was definitively,
and Squirrel would have appreciated this, off-message.

So Kyle had decided he would not let them exploit the
accident for their gain. He'd taken Squirrel's keys, visited the
Justice League offices that morning, and absconded with the
briefcase.

"He's from Pikeville," Kyle said.

"Ah, the rural East," Barr said. "You'll have to be patient
with her."

"She doesn't know who he is."

Kyle looked over at Barr. His rumpled dress shirt and red
mesh sports shorts made him seem half undressed already.
Judging by the topography, Kyle was pretty sure he was free-
balling. Barr had the ferocious calves of a shot-putter—a
coachlike solidity that Kyle would never admit stirred him.
Barr had shaved his head down to a fringe of black hair, and
his face had a serene, almost baked quality from years of comfortable executive living or a long drip of hard alcohol. But a
loneliness pervaded the house, a single man in a mansion.

Barr stared back and Kyle detected a not-unfamiliar
searching, undefended quality. Since Kyle had moved to
Kentucky—the only person he knew to *move* there and not
grow up there, like some hothouse flower—he'd come to know
that a goodly portion of the gay men in Kentucky were, in fact,
married to women. It was a Southern fact. He'd met them at
bars *with their rings on*. The contradiction was part of their
appeal, maybe all of it—Lord knows, the pleated pants were

not. He even had gay friends back in Philly who advertised online as straight and married because it worked. Men wanted a challenge, a conquest, terrain where they could plant a flag.

"So you're not an activist?" Barr asked. "What's your line of work then?"

Kyle had several answers to this, but the honest one was staring at the ceiling, trying to will a professional life into being. His relationship with Squirrel had introduced him to penniless activists who were not impressed by full-bleed layouts. They'd rather xerox a xerox, samizdats for a cool war, and look at him with pity. At least in Philly he'd designed album covers, websites for nonprofits, and if he wasn't paid well or wasn't paid at all, at least they'd been grateful. The looming truth was that he'd have to reboot: move back to Philly and be broke there.

"I'm between jobs," Kyle answered. "And let's put jobs in quotes."

Barr said then that he wanted to propose something, and that if Kyle didn't like what he heard, he could get up and go and there would be no consequences. This was the opening Kyle could see coming miles away. It didn't shock him. Not anymore. Not living in the northernmost Southern state, where gentlemen preferred their piece on the side to be preppy, discreet. He drained his glass and smiled to himself in the dark.

"I have a job for you," Barr said. "And Kyle, listen, you could be a real game-changer."

5.

The arrangement was this: the boy would return on Saturday afternoon to mow the back lawn, some demonstrable work for the pay. But it was after that Leland waited for, when he would make them a drink, they would sit in the mottled light of the gazebo, and the young man would report back on the meetings of the Mountain Justice League.

At first, Kyle was cagey and hesitant. He wasn't sure what Leland wanted to know, or why, and the details he offered were digressive, more color than anything. Like the injured boy's progress—he remained in the rehab unit of the hospital, struggling to regain his speech. Or the various fund-raising farragoes: an upcoming occupation of a city park, or the decision to raise money for a single mother in a godforsaken hollow who had run afoul of the banks. Leland didn't care about good works. He wanted to understand the bull's-eye—who drew it, where it would be. The leading edge of their campaigns. Kyle left with cash, two hundred dollars a visit. After the first time, Leland wasn't sure the boy would return. But then, there he was the following Saturday at four, in a baseball cap, headphones in his ears. And again the next Saturday, when he asked for two hundred and fifty, and Leland did not balk.

"You realize they're just kids," Kyle said, folding the money into the breast-pocket of his shirt. "I could tell you about the lentil-loaf recipes and twinkle hands for consensus. But I'm pretty sure you don't give a shit."

Leland did not. But he had, without knowing it, come to

anticipate this time. The utter improbability: a young stranger, feet up on a rattan ottoman like he owned the place, sharing a drink with him in the shade. Leland's world had become a strict dial of interactions—his secretary's chilly regard, an unseen lawyer faxing him divorce paperwork, and site managers reporting in—none of which provoked him in any discernable direction. His physician had told him to smile if no other reason than it softened the ventricles of the heart. So Leland smiled.

Leland said, "I've come to see you as a friend." Was that true? It was. The young man was his only regular company.

"Do you pay all your friends?" Kyle asked.

"I think we pay each other in different ways."

Kyle stretched his back with his hands planted at the top of his ass. A sort of bowing, throwing his midriff forward, pulling his shirt up at his waist, revealing the smooth, carved joint at the top of his thigh. It was a move that heterosexual men did not, could not, do. A strange stirring alit inside Leland. It had been months since he had been touched, his body a map he skipped over: the ridgeline of hair on his shoulder that Merrill had once asked him to shave, his belly that bulged like a dumpling . . . What did the boy see? He tried and the image was blank.

"Restroom?" Kyle asked.

Leland pointed at the back door.

"Or can I pee outside like a wild animal?" His eyes were unwavering, drawing something from Leland.

"Feel free," Leland said. The boy grinned and slipped his feet back his shoes. A performance was beginning, and Leland discovered he was a willing audience. Kyle opened the screen door and paused.

"Hey, so, what is the Dominion Project?" Kyle said. "They mentioned it at the meeting. Something Origin was trying to do. Buy up a whole bunch of mountains. That King was just the first."

Leland circled the ice in his glass. An insect drowned at the bottom. How had it made its way in? The gazebo was screened.

"It's better if you know less," Leland said.

How much he, too, would rather know less. Origin Resources intended to dragline a significant portion of Lawrence County's choicest seams; he would like to unknow that. The spoil rock they sent into streams was not harmless, incidental. The numbers were not good numbers. As a boy, Leland once imagined he would become a veterinarian, a savior to the animals—the kind of thing you imagined yourself *as* but never being, master of the vital operations and desperate rescues of what we actually love. Instead, he knew extraction.

Kyle looked out at the lawn and seemed to resign himself to his answer. Leland adjusted his seat cushion. The screen door slammed into its frame as Kyle walked across the lawn to the house and never returned.

6.

The basket of soaps, the "Bless This House" wooden carving on the wall of the bathroom: a woman had been here, Kyle thought, but a woman had also bolted and left the geegaws. The toilet roll had run out. The medicine cabinet seemed raided. It was as though Barr, too, was subtracting himself from the place. Maybe this is what made him diffuse, or desperate to have someone to drink with. It surprised Kyle that Barr had not already busted a move, given the private nature of a screened-in sex gazebo. He kept waiting for the other shoe to drop, for the wandering hand, for the lurching kiss, no doubt with snake tongue. Maybe Kyle'd be wrong, and the pretext of back channel about the Mountain Justice people was, in fact, just the text. Maybe Barr had no ulterior motive. Or maybe Kyle was supposed to make the first overture. Some prostitutes got paid just to hang out, didn't they? Was that what he was, an almost-sex worker? The feeling was exotic and, he had to admit, credentializing.

He finished pissing and wandered the ground floor of the house. The dining room was missing the table and chairs, so a chandelier hung over a rug. A leather armchair ruled the center of a sunroom, a scattering of papers around the base. He saw the legions of bottles, an empty, plaid dog bed, so much empty. In the kitchen, on the marble island, was Barr's laptop, playing the endless pipe screen saver.

Then Kyle stopped. On the counter was Squirrel's blue bandana, folded into a square, with coins on top. What the fuck was this doing here? How had Barr not seen fit to give it to him, the only person to whom it would matter? Kyle took it and held it up to his face. Squirrel's scent was gone, the cotton laundered. A memory came: Squirrel's terrified face on

the ground, one bloodshot eye, not understanding how irrevocable the day had become. He would never be the same, a
venturesome boy on the edge of a dozer blade.

Kyle looked back out to the gazebo, where Barr awaited,
and felt the grip of a new loyalty take hold.

7.

It was early morning on the mountain, the sky gray and bil-
lowy. They'd have rain and the site would turn into a swamp.
In the office, sitting across from Leland in a creaky wheeled
chair, the site manager took off his sunglasses and pinched at
the bridge of his nose. "Leland, just tell me if I'll have a job in
three months." Leland had no answer.

He left him and fled, down the ridge, boots crunching
through the shale.

Two mornings back, the paper had started publishing
everything—the extraction numbers, the data on the looming
nitrogen levels in the creek beds, the next run of mountains.
All taken from his laptop, gone missing, after that afternoon
with the boy. Origin stock had already started its slide, and the
television would run their first report that evening. The board
figured a leak inside the company, and secretaries had been
let go. But it was only a matter of time before it got traced
back to Leland. He was convinced now that the encounter had
been plotted. What could he say, to anyone? That he hired a
spy. Even Merrill had called him, concerned about the news

stories, but he stopped answering. He was alone now, at the bottom of a hole with his mistake.

Leland came to the clearing where the oak tree remained on its side, the leaves brown and the root-ball dry. He noticed names carved in its bark, initials and other lettering that ringed the trunk. People had been here once and left their mark. The tracks of the dozer remained in the dirt, the place where the boy fell. The grasses in the cemetery were beginning to explode without the canopy to starve them. And nearby was an older woman with a shovel and bundled tarp on the ground who watched him with suspicion. Her long gray hair had been pulled into a ponytail and she wore a T-shirt printed with what looked like the photo of a cat.

"I know who you are," she said. "Go get away now."

But Leland moved toward her. The siren blared back at the site. The two-minute hazard warning. A long orange chain of fuses, like a braid of Christmas lights, were set into drill holes sixty feet deep. Fly rock would shower. The tremor could shatter an ankle.

"Didn't you hear me?" she said.

The grave markers were mostly broken, mossy remnants. Her small stone was one of the newest, a piece of granite with "DOLLOP" chiseled crudely into the rock. A green collar lay on the stone. It was a pet cemetery. A shaft inside him collapsed in: she was going to dig up her animal. You could never know what mattered to someone else, or how much. The thing was: to matter at all.

"Is this your cat?" Leland asked. "Let me help."

She grimaced. "You have no idea what you done."

It was then he saw, underneath the tarp, the branches. The roots bundled in muslin and twine. It was a sapling behind her, laid sidelong. She was going to set the tree in the earth, give the grave some shade.

But then the blast cap fired and his feet felt the rumble first. The bang echoed, like a gunshot, into the valley. A dank smell, the spent fuses, materialized in the air around them. The mountain, finally, was open.

When You Are the Final Girl

Nobody wants to know where monsters come from. But I know. Because I am one. They come from a soundproof room, beige and white, with a door that seals for positive oxygen flow. Monsters come from all around to be born there, in the pure oxygen. Still, the place smells like Vaseline and burnt toast.

Outside the room are six beds, hidden by curtains. There, the nurses put cadaver skin on you because it has nutrients your monster skin needs. An Asian nurse lady, the one who wasn't afraid, laid gray pieces of dead guy on my face. When her fingers patted the gauze, I heard a scream. It came from me, a gust from inside, but I couldn't find where.

She gave me drugs to forget my life before, as a person. But the drugs stopped words from having beginnings and endings, so I got what was in between: giant vowels, jets of breath. My mother brought me magazines and my music. I could only put the earphones in one ear, the ear that remained, but music saved me. Movie soundtracks saved me. "Randy, I need to tell you something," my mother said. "He's here. He's in the building." The boy that made me a monster was on another floor, getting saved. I asked the nurse to push as much forgetting into me as she could.

"You're going to feel an itch soon," the nurse lady said. She was a hundred years old and every one of those years she'd taken the bus. But her fingers were soft, the only fingers that I allowed. "When you feel it, you should think far away," she said. "Think of your favorite place." I thought of my last night as a person, in the mall parking lot, and Melissa Carmichael's lap, Melissa whom I barely knew, who never came to see me. Good-bye, Melissa.

After a week, a baby monster came. She had crawled into a heating vent and got stuck, pressed against hot metal. It's dangerous to give babies the drugs, but she shrieked so much the doctors gave them anyway. Then she got quiet and I heard, through the curtain, the clicks and the wheeze of a bike pump going all night. At some point, the pump stopped and her mother gasped and wept. Maybe she should've fixed the vent. All of a sudden, I was crying too, except it felt like my face was tearing apart, like a paper bag I was done with. That was when my itch came, hot and unrelenting. Next day, the nurses had to tie down my hands.

One day, my mother brought me the newspaper. She put her hand on my arm and said, "He's dead, Randy. It's right here." His high school portrait, right above the funeral notice. They'd tried lots of things but his heart gave. My mother let the smallest smile happen. I saw every muscle doing its work.

Right after, I told the nurses to stop the drugs. It was time to go home, to remember my life. Except now, like every monster, I've got two arrows in my head: one going forward to what I want, and the other going back to what made me. These arrows move at the same speed, in different directions, and trying to hold them both in your head will make anybody crazy.

Is a horror story a horror story if the monster tells it?

A row of store-bought superheroes, cowgirls, and witches line up at the entrance of the Rutland Firehouse, waiting to be scared. In the parking lot, adults in parent costumes lean against cars and blow air into their fists. Tonight is Halloween. I have my hair back in a ponytail. My costume is a sign around my neck that says "Go Ahead and Stare."

On a branch at the edge of the car lot, a yellowed medical skeleton dangles, and a punk comes and snaps the last nob of coccyx. The air is a freezer door open to my face, and the cold makes the itch. Heat, sweat, cold, tears, smiling: they all make the itch. When that happens, I have to busy my hands. I press them onto the warm hood of my car, but I'm nervous and my hands won't heat.

Jess isn't here yet. Jess will warm things.

"Look at this," Solvang says. "This one will rock you."

He flips a playing card onto the hood. For the past three months, over cheese and onion sandwiches at lunch, Solvang has been giving me dispatches about this newest project, a deck of cards he designed. He works at the printing office next to Kramer Photo and Retouch, where I'm at, and he has access to the machines. After hours, he prints up these cards, each with a disturbing image, gore from the Internet that no one should see: crime scenes, blade accidents, amputees doing stuff. Solvang spent his childhood in the northern territories, in a one-room cabin with his parents, backwoods Swedes who taught him that life is about having something to trade. The latest: a girl tucked in the fetal position, lying in pink soup.

"Guess," he says.

"A kid in a big purse," I say.

"Not even close."

"I don't want to know," says Callie, Solvang's wife. "Those cards are evil." With one hand, she forks her fingers into her hair, and with the other, she rains glitter. During the day, when she's not taking care of their baby son, Callie housecleans for a B&B up on the ski mountain. Tonight, she's a fairy godmother, in a busty silver gown and tiara. She was Wiccan for a while, so she knows how to accessorize. Her magic wand is a curtain rod with a tinfoil ball at the end, but I'm getting more of a scepter feel.

"That is a python," Solvang says, "with a girl inside it."

I pinch Callie's foil into star points. "I thought that was the other one."

"That one was an orca," he says, "with a dude inside it." He flips to the next: a Siamese cat crammed inside a bottle, face against the glass. Somebody trimmed its whiskers and it looks so not psyched. "Check it," he says. "The bonsai kitten. The cat lives in the bottle its whole life. They blow pot in its face to runt it."

"Can we talk about something else?" Callie interrupts. "Something normal?"

A boy in a hospital gown approaches us, trailing his dad. The kid has a bleeding scar on his forehead, piecrust and red coloring dye. It looks carefully worked over.

"Excuse me but your face looks amazing," he says to me. "How did you do it?"

His father takes his hand. "He loves horror movies, sorry." I lean down to the kid, my cardboard sign dangling. I want him to be able to see up close, no flinching. "It's not a costume," I say.

The kid blinks, confused. His father forces a laugh and then jerks his son toward the line, like what I've got might be able to be given.

"So how much longer do we have to wait?" Callie says. "The posters said eight o'clock. It's been eight o'clock for a year."

Tonight is Eddie Cosimano's show—his name was all over the poster. "Horror effects by FX wizard Eddie Cosimano (*Rumplestiltskin II, The Witching of Amanda Jane*)." I know Eddie from high school, when we worked in the audio-visual room, shuttling the TV carts. During study periods, we watched horror movies over and over. The classics, the remakes and reboots, the Japanese ones that start as romantic comedies then turn to vivisection. All of them. Right after graduation, Eddie went out to California to work in film, but you have to freeze-frame to catch his name in the credits. He'd come back to Rutland to "regroup." One guy. He gets to regroup.

"I'm cold," Callie says. "Somebody warm me up." Solvang rubs her shoulders, then nestles in for a kiss. He purses his lips like he's drinking from a faucet, like she's a necessary element,

and Callie moans a little. I still don't know what that feels like.
I so want to know.

Just then, a van with tinted windows pulls into the lot,
brights in our faces. The line of kids kinks around it, chattering at the arrival. When the driver-side door opens, mist
billows out to the ground. My heart seizes a bit to know just
how far Eddie has taken this. A black boot descends, buck-
led to the knee, and Eddie steps from the driver's chair, in an
overcoat and a cap that says "*R II*." His beard has crop circles.
He takes a scan of the crowd and then hits the unlock. Here's
where things get interesting, where things get different. The
back doors open and a posse of vampire girls stretch their legs
and follow. Last to emerge is Jess, the stake in my heart, the
answer for everything. Her face is powdered to alabaster. Her
eyes and lips, coal black. A charcoal cape doesn't quite cover
her blouse. She wears a plaid, pleated skirt and ripped white
leggings. She's all Catholic School except for two gray fangs.
She stumbles a bit, unsure where to go until Eddie whisks her
inside.

The itch says, Careful. My right hand dives in my shirt
pocket to make sure the pills haven't moved. All there, safe
and unsound, a handful of white roofies for the partner of my
choosing. No more waiting. Tonight, I'm Jack with the magic
beans. Here comes the stalk. Here comes the climb up into
the clouds.

Jess stood at the door of Kramer Photo in her remember-me
best: a tight blue V-neck sweater, brown hair curtaining around

her face, and J.C. on the cross nestled between her Temple Mounts. It was the same outfit she had had on before, in her first round of pictures.

"I'm here for my retakes?" she said.

"You're an hour late," I said from the door, giving her my good side. She ran J.C. up and down on his chain.

"Sorry," Jess said, and shrugged. "Student Council."

For six weeks in the fall, portraits from all over the county flood into Kramer Photo. October is yearbook season. I work in the back and out of view, retouching—clearing complexions, subtracting acne from the record. You wouldn't guess, considering, that I am good at this particular fix. But I had the job before the accident, and Kramer kept me on after. "Nobody else looks as close as you do," he said. And he's right. I see all the way to the pore. The measly flare, the third-eye keloid. Our skin is where we're judged, first and last.

I brought Jess upstairs to the studio. The door locked behind her.

Kramer and the others had already left, so it was just us in the studio. I had spent time prepping and figuring how to shade the space. She'd stay under the brights and flashes, and I'd stay behind the lens until she blacked out. The shades were drawn, but the studio felt cool and outdoorsy—that was the "Forest Glade" on the wall, a twelve-foot scrim of birch and fallen leaves. For portrait backgrounds, Kramer offers "Star Field," "42nd Street," and "Forest Glade."

"I made you some coffee," I said. I pointed to the cup, right there on the light table. Extra strong, to mask the dose.

"No thanks," she said.

"Soda? No soda?" I offered. "Or something harder?"

I'd already had two shots myself before her arrival, to quiet my nerves. But she shook her head. At some point, girls learn they don't have to answer every question. And like that, my plan, the careful order of things, guttered out.

Jess spun on the stool while I adjusted the lights. Kramer specializes in large format, big prints, everything adjustable. Through the viewfinder, her face was a dish of cream. Her two front teeth had a slot between them for the perfect dime. No blemishes—somehow she'd made it that far without scars. I would barely need to retouch.

"I feel like I'm in a diorama with this forest thing behind me," she said. "I should have a papoose and a spear."

"Didn't your form say Forest Glade?" I said.

"I had nothing to do with the form," she said. "My mother was all about the form."

I felt a strange possessive surge. I didn't want her known or noticed, possessed by a family. When you come this far, this close, the aperture closes around what you see, and you want to be the only one looking. I tested the flash. The recharging whine rose to the top of the sound register. She asked if we lost other yearbook photos along with hers.

"I bet a lot of kids want to take theirs again," she said.

"Sure, but you don't want to peak when you're seventeen," I said. "You don't want to be fifty and look at the Rutland High School yearbook like those were the good days."

"If I'm looking at my yearbook when I'm fifty," she said,

"claw my eyes out." Then she thought for a moment and took J.C. off her neck and laid him on the light table.

"Got plans for Halloween?" I asked.

She told me about Eddie's invitation, duly noted. My plan floated back from oblivion. I'd find her then.

"So what is his deal? Is he gay?" she asked. "Because he asked me to be a vampire and supposedly he's amazing with makeup."

"He's not gay, he's just really into base," I said. She laughed then and it was like she released herself to me.

"Ready?" I said.

The smile is always the hard part, because it has nothing to do with the mouth. It's all in the eyes. A grin lifted into her face, but it was only in the bottom half, what happens when you live with something.

"Thanks," she said on the way out, taking the stairs two at a time. "Make me look beautiful, okay?"

Inside the Halloween firehouse, the light drops. I make out a long hallway of black-lit paintings and one cheap, low-hanging bat that won't last the night. Then the hallway opens out onto the kitchen where a kid lies under a sheet on a table. On cue, a chainsaw cranks and Dewey Church—the guy who trims everybody's trees—steps out from behind the door. The sound is deafening, and Solvang covers Callie's ears. Dewey plows through the belly of the screaming kid, sending an outrageous spray and guts into the air. Solvang casually picks a piece off his flack jacket. Baked ziti. The chainsaw quiets and the disemboweled kid dips his hands into the gash to eat some. Dewey knocks the side of his head.

"Don't play with your guts, you idiot."

"But it's freaky," the kid says.

"It's confusing," Dewey says. "Your dying moments, and you're going to taste yourself?"

The next room is a nonstarter. A pack of twelve-year-olds dolled up like zombies—Eddie really went for the coolie labor here—wander around and bump into each other. A preteen ghoul clings to us, almost like he's angling for change. Callie shoves him away, but I corral the kid before he can slink off.

"Why did she push me?" The kid repaves his bald cap.

"Because you were poking her."

"I'm supposed to poke," he says. "Eddie told me to poke."

He tells me Eddie is on the roof, and we zip through the rest of the building: more kids leaping out from behind chairs, mattresses. The longhair manager from Video King, way too old for the room, proudly wears a diarrhea-ass costume from Spencer Gifts, leaking all over the place. In a shower, a chick dressed in a white sheet plays a harp. Solvang fixes on her and the girl waves back. Callie pulls him on.

"Who was that?" she demands.

"I don't know," Solvang says.

Callie knocks him on the head with her wand. "You know her."

"Jesus," he says. "Your fucking wand fucking hurts."

Out the back, past the exit, I catch the murmuring up on the roof. A training staircase runs up the back of the building, to the promising noise. Jess has to be up there. When I ask Solvang and Callie if they want to crash the party, they do that couple-deciding thing, where she's looking to see what he wants and he's looking to see what she wants and it takes five minutes for them to decide that they're too tired to go out. But for once, Callie is game. "What's at home?" she says. "Let the babysitter deal."

The roof is the size of the community pool. A cloud of dope hangs over the proceedings. At the other end, groupies circle Eddie while he boasts that he "made over a thousand dollars in the first hour." His jaw chomps and chomps, with some chemistry of his own.

I see Jess, propped up on the edge of the roof, imprinting the lip of a Styrofoam cup with her fangs. Her pupils are big as volume knobs—Eddie must have fit her with black contacts.

"Mr. Randy DiSilva!" Eddie calls out to me. "Buddy, been way too long." He waves me over and claps me on the back. Then he tilts his head and examines my face as if I'm auditioning.

"What'd you use?" he says. "Latex glue?"

"For what?"

"For this," he says, running his finger down the left side of his face, eye to his chin. He has no idea.

I shake my head. "No, latex."

"Gelatin?" He asks.

"Glass," I go. "Some fire."

I let that sink, but Eddie's too juiced to follow. "Huh?"

Solvang shows up, changing the subject. "So, Randy, is Amanda Jane here?"

"The girl from the stupid movie?" Eddie says. "Oh, yeah, right, she's doing Ouija by the keg."

Solvang scans for her and Callie watches him look for this girl, the girl who's not her, and it pains me. She's loyal to him the way people get when they start feeding a feral animal, leaving a plate out, expecting the animal to care. Solvang was raised in the woods. He'll go back there eventually. I know they're having trouble—Solvang told me that he can't get it up since he saw her making way for the baby. "I just keep expecting other stuff to keep coming out," he told me. "It's your playing cards," I told him. "They're rotting you."

I peel off from Eddie and head to the drinks. I pump two beers into red plastic cups and mash one of my pills on the edge of the table. It doesn't quite powder and it gets in the foam, but I stir it in with a finger. She doesn't need much. Jess looks up, blank and unfocused, when I approach. The itch starts up, with the sweat.

"Jess," I go. "It's me, the guy who took your portrait the other day."

"Randy, right?" she says. Maybe the friendliness takes a little too long to shape into her face, but we'll get there. Her lips don't know what to do with the fangs, so they rest on the outside, like a rabbit. "I'm sorry. I can't see anything. These contacts are driving me crazy."

"I brought you a beer," I say. She takes it, but it goes nowhere near her lips. "So what's your costume?"

"I came as normal," I say. "The boy next door."

She nods. "Oh that's a hard one, that one takes time," she says. The fingers have been snipped off her gloves, and with bluing fingers, she accordions the pleats in her skirt. Her knees are right there, offered through the rips in her leggings. The itch says, *Start there.*

She holds out her hand. "You want this?" she says. A mint-colored pill rests in her palm, a fish-tank pebble. "Eddie gave it to me and told me it was aspirin."

I have competition. I sit next to her on the edge. "That's not aspirin."

"It figures," she says. "He's a creepster."

"Have you seen his movies?"

"I watched like ten minutes of the one about the imp and the spell and the whatever."

"So why'd you sign up to join the vampire squad?"

"He said I could die in his next one," she says. "Gotta start somewhere."

"Maybe one day you'll get to be the final girl," I say.

Jess squeezes up her face. "She's the one who never has sex, right? Because when you have sex in those movies you die."

"The final girl is the last one alive, that's all that matters," I say. "The beautiful one nobody notices, except we do, the audience. She's the one with the inner resources and the keys and the journey and the one weird implement that brings death. Chopsticks. Or the poker. Or hair spray on fire. And then at the end, when she looks over the railing, or into the pit, that's the abyss looking into her. And she's alive. And her being alive means we're alive."

You don't need to be all that smart. You just have to make the girl feel like she gives off light.

"You watch a lot of movies, Randy," she says, and it's so much specialness that it distracts me from asking how she knows my name.

I'd just ruined the Bronco twins. Two cowlicky bullies from East Rutland whose princely poses I saw and went, *Here are two people who deserve some damage.* All it took was a little more cherry and less nude in the paintbrush. When I was done, Kenny Bronco looked like a flaming leper.

So I didn't notice her at first. I almost passed her prints straight into the shipment. Almost. But then I took her in: the blue sweater, the brown hair, that crucifix nestled at the base of her neck. Her skin was trophy golden. She seemed familiar, like a sequel.

And then it wasn't her face I was seeing, but a face I've seen so many times in my head that he's my Forest Glade. Her brother's face, in the obituaries. My mother had kept the page for me until after I was out of the hospital and could focus. Eric Denning, seventeen. He'd started his own lawn-mowing company and was planning, like half of everybody, on getting the hell out of Rutland. I was too, before I became a monster.

I went to Kramer's catalog to confirm what I already knew: the photo in my hand was Jessica Denning. I never knew your brother, Jessica. But five years ago, drunk and bored, he bent time around me. He crossed the yellow line and splintered my life in two.

I took the digital files and dragged them into the trash. My pulse jumped when Kramer came into the room. He dove into the office fridge.

"Hey, boss, we're missing this one girl's prints," I said. "Can't find her in the bin. Some kind of error in the camera?"

Kramer popped open his soda. "Just schedule her for next week, then," he said. "She's all yours."

Suddenly, sirens. Down below, in the firehouse parking lot, two police cars pull up. The blue and right lights make everybody on the roof wave the air to waft away the dope smell which, for about five seconds, seems like an idea. Then everybody runs. Eddie hitches his pants, heads to the stairs. "Remember the legend of Edward Cosimano!" he shouts.

"Cops are here," I tell her.

"Are you serious?" she says. She tugs her cape in close. "I can't see."

Solvang crashes into us, throwing one arm around me. "Hey, you—you should love this guy," he says to her. "Randy is ready for love." I'd like to kill him right now. I see Solvang dead on a punji stick, like one of his cards.

Callie comes and catches him. He got in a drinking contest with one of the zombies, she says. Jess snaps off her fangs and says, "Let's go."

Sometimes you walk up to a wall and you walk through.

I lope with Solvang's arm around my shoulder, and we work our way down the stairs until we're ground level. Out front, I can hear Eddie arguing with the cops. Cars tear out of the lot, nipping past us. I dump Solvang in the backseat of my car. When I turn around, Callie is wiping her mouth with a bit of her gown. There's a grim puddle at her feet.

"I think I just vomited," Callie says, without surprise.

Jess steps around. "Shotgun."

We drive in quiet. As we pull into Callie and Solvang's driveway, their babysitter fumes on the wooden stairs. "I have been waiting for hours," she goes. "I was supposed to be at a rave at ten."

Solvang twists out the door and just spills. The babysitter, disgusted, hops on her ten-speed. "The kid's asleep—if you care," she says, and goes.

For a moment, we just sit there. "I'm pregnant," Callie goes, into her hands. "I know nobody cares. I just thought somebody should know."

Nobody says a word. I walk Solvang back to the house with Callie trailing behind in the silence she made. Their place is a mess, like the baby is doing the arranging. Life-size cutouts of WWF wrestling guys—Solvang is a fan—circle their living room, peopling it with goons. I roll Solvang off onto the bed in the master bedroom. It's a waterbed, and the wave action sounds like a stomach digesting.

Solvang is a little gray in the lips. He wakes up some and pulls my head toward his, mumbling. Somebody gave him a pill on the roof, he says. One of Eddie's aspirins. Then he takes my hand and rests it on his hard-on. He's proud, like it's a science project that managed to work after all.

"That's the proof," he says, bleary.

"Proof of what?"

"Proof I'm not dead."

In the kitchen, Callie sits at their tiny table, a young crone. She plays with her wand, remolds the star points that have blunted.

"Callie, I'm sorry, but I've got to go," I say.

She taps her wand once against her belly. "Bing," she says. "All gone." Back at the car, Jess's working on her eyes, trying to fish out the contacts. The rip at her knee, I swear, is bigger.

"I can't get these things out," she says. "And now it's kind of scaring me."

"Where am I taking you?" I ask.

She stops for a minute. "Not home," she says. "Not yet."

Just three folding chairs in twenty feet square. I was four months into my treatment, pacing the clinic courtyard. The walls of the courtyard were glass and with noonday sun, we got our reflections back. The heat made the itch so I couldn't stay in the sun for long. I pressed my fingers on the left side of my face to feel out the tender parts. My face looked like somebody fried an egg there and forgot about it. I looked like something you'd never want to look at.

"So what happened to the other guy?" I heard behind me.

He was in jeans and sunglasses, sitting in one of the folding chairs kicked back on its rear two legs. He was a tree cowboy, one of the loggers from upstate, compact and hardy. But from the collar of his shirt rose a bright red welt, up his neck, onto his jaw.

"Sorry?" I said.

"The other guy," the cowboy asked. "The guy that hit you in his car. The nurses talk."

"He died," I said.

The man nodded. "My ex-wife set my house on fire," he said. "Since then, I've been coming back here. They take pieces of me and move them around so I can look like everybody else."

He held up a hand that had the fingers fused together. "I ain't never going to look like everybody else," he said. "Neither will you."

He banged his chair back to the ground so he could dig around in his pocket with his good hand. He found a blister pack of pills. No label or markings.

"How old are you?"

"Twenty-two," I said.

He tossed the packet at me. "Take some of those."

"What are they?"

"They're not for you. They're for her."

"For who?"

"For the girl," he said. "For the partner of your choosing."

I shake my head and hand the pills back. "No thank you."

He scratched at his cheek and considered what came next. "Listen to me. I'm doing you a favor. You're broken now. Just like every person who comes through here. No woman is going to look at you. You'll see. You've got lots of time, lots of time to see what I'm saying. The only kind of sex you'll have, from here on out, is up in your head."

He must have seen something shift in me. Because he tossed those pills right back.

The Star Mart, it figures, doesn't have a bathroom. So I huddle by the magazine rack, crushing two pills against the shelf, Jess waiting in the car. I won't miss this time. I pour the powder from my hand into the neck of a soda bottle and shake it. When I pay, the Indian at the counter gives me a look. Behind him, a bank of security camera feeds. There's one over the magazine rack. He saw everything, says nothing.

Back in the car, I set the bottle between us. "Thirsty?" I say. "I got us a soda."

"Let's go somewhere," she says, taking the bottle.

So I drive to the deserted Rutland Mid-City Mall. It's been waiting for demolition for years. You can look in the windows and see rolls of carpet and dummies and florescent bulbs. In the acres of asphalt and lamplight, you feel like you're parked on the moon. I used to come here and join up with a crowd of smokers on the backside, where we'd turned a patch of curb into our spot.

"This place is special for me," I say. It was here that I met this beautiful girl, Melissa Carmichael, in a skirt and with a scarf on her wrist. Melissa was up from the Berkshires, the only one of us not getting stoned. I lay my head in her lap and told her about my favorite soundtracks. She combed my hair with her fingers and loved me in minutes. But then she had to go, she said, she was staying with a friend. "When can I see you? I have to see you," I said, and she told me she would come back tomorrow tonight except Eric Denning found me that night and then I never saw her again.

"This is where I last felt like a person," I say.

Jess blinks slowly, preparing to speak. "My brother wanted to draw comic books," she says. "I kept all his drawings."

She knows who I am. She peels the label off the bottle. Half of it's already gone.

"Once I came to visit you in the hospital," she says. "I was eleven. And I went by myself. I was so scared." She smears the black eye shadow with the back of her hand. "They wouldn't let me see you." Her hand moves toward me, searching for mine. "I'm sorry."

I flinch. "Don't."

Already, she's going slack. I wonder how big a dose I put in there, how long she's going to be out.

"I'm feeling sick," she says.

Then she's gone, pillowed against the door. Her chest rises and falls even and regular. Her breath frosts a white cloud on the window. Her cell phone rings. Someone's looking for her. I undo my seatbelt. It takes some doing, but I press my head where it belongs, into her lap, into a warm invitation. I want to keep her like this for a long time.

Curious Father

Yes, Henry would like to say something.

In the early part of his marriage, Henry started an extension to the house that he never finished. Ten years and counting, conduit still sprouts from the ceiling. Pink ribs of insulation are just there. His wife, Margot, made him put in a twin bed to home it up. She was afraid their daughter Effie would go and electrocute herself, fork in socket, to a curly-haired cinder. But Effie didn't go into the room, because she thought it was haunted, and in a way, it was. Eventually, there was this door they didn't talk about and never went into.

Then, one morning this spring, Margot opened it. This was right after her test results came back negative, and she was all about new patterns. Like soy milk and morning Zumba and finishing the unfinished. She moved the bed to clean and Henry heard the crash of his magazines and videotapes. His body tensed in the magnifying quiet. At the state concert hall in New Brunswick, where he works as a stage manager, he's heard a soloist's violin crack and fold in from pressure. He's seen the lighting grid come raining.

Irrevocable things happen all the time.

Henry rose and found her on the edge of mattress, leafing

through his porn, his secret cache. Men in the photos, mouths
and bodies penetrated on every page. At her feet, she'd made
a neat stack of the videos, the sad lot of them, whose titles—
Fuckbuds, Dungeon Cops, The Delights of Allan Twinkler—
gave Henry's shame a fresh edge.

"Just tell me," Margot said, "did these do you any good?"
And at that moment, before it got bad and then worse,
while they still had their patterns (a little sun of grapefruit
in the morning, a joint each month on date night), Henry
was more in love with her than he'd ever been. Love like
she was the last log of a splintering raft. Henry was, and still
is, terrified.

Six months later, Margot's therapist e-mails Henry's therapist a link. "Dawn Manor," the website reads. "When it's
time to get found." On the website, a group of men sling
their arms over each other like a softball team. Honestly,
Henry prefers a little more space between people. This
manor, a big Victorian in the Catskills, is a kind of workshop
for "men who love men" but are bent out of shape about
it. Henry can't find anybody close to his age in the photos,
but he never sees people his age in advertisements unless
they're for pills or Florida. On the "Who We Are" page, in a
portrait staged with professional light, two men with iden-
tical goatees press their heads together with a golden retriever between them. "Dawn Manor is operated by author/
certified intuitive Bodi Charles," the caption reads, "and his
husband Spike and dog Rigby."

"His husband," Henry says to himself, trying it out, and decides it sounds absurd. At fifty-three-years-old, with readers and a disconcertingly white thatch of hair on his chest, he'll be lucky to land a fuckbud. Now that his secret life, furtive visits to the Lion's Den adult bookstore, terrified opportunism in public restrooms, has become his actual one, he sees he has chosen to die horny and alone.

Tonight, his best friend Van, the sound engineer at the concert hall, is coming over to "christen the escape pod," he said. They've been friends for years, and lovers in Henry's mind for nearly as long. At work, the production crew calls Van "the Pirate" on account of his hoop earring and his grizzle along the jaw; the nickname alone brings Henry's cheery erection out of early retirement. Van wears construction boots with the laces so loose they're really flip-flops. Everything he keeps on him—wallet, watch, Leatherman—is hitched to his belt with metal links, so none of his needs can get too far from him. Van is just about forty and newly divorced. His son visits on weekends. Henry is lonely enough not to care that he's in love with a straight man.

"I like the Christmas lights," Van says on arrival, taking in the studio. "Very bachelor Noël."

Van wears a blazer and a cap that reads "VOLUNTEER" across the front; this visit, it occurs to Henry, may be a form of community service. Under his arm, Van carries a radio with a broken antennae that "gets angry" if you play with it too much. "From my divorce to yours," Van says, leaning back in the other chair.

"Beer?" Henry asks.

Van shakes his head and asks for a soda. "I'm sober these days, chief."

When Henry hired him, Van had been a mess. Van showed up at work with bloodshot eyes, lazy about feedback. Henry sensed around him a general state of transition, and he felt compelled to know it, join it, as if he himself were there, choosing his life all over again. Earlier this year, when Van's car got repo'd—a negotiation in the settlement had gone sour—Henry picked him up and drove him home, an errand that became the high point of his days. With his feet propped on the dash like a boy, Van would monologue about how bad his divorce had become. What Henry truly remembered, in a way that he was only beginning to understand, was the dark prairie of hair on Van's forearm, the surf at his collar: the places on men that he only now allows himself to see.

Henry dances the salt and pepper shakers in his hands for an hour, angling up to his confession. It is difficult to be honest with the people you find beautiful.

"I feel about twenty years late to this, but I think I just finally found out I am . . ." Henry says, "someone who is . . ."

"Gay," Van says with a sly grin.

"Was it that obvious?"

"Come on, it's *theater*. Everybody's gay. Or at least tried out the buffet." This alights Henry's sense of an opening. He feels relieved and vulnerable, newborn.

Van digs in the fridge. "I'll have that beer now." When Henry shows surprise, Van shrugs. "Special occasions."

They talk, rambling their way to midnight. On his departure, Van hugs him and Henry registers that a man has never held him so forcefully, so intimately. The sheer surface area nearly makes him puddle. "Congratulations," Van says into his ear, and his hot breath makes new weather across Henry's interior life. "You'll never have boring sex again."

Effie comes by Henry's apartment with throw rugs, donuts, and a scented candle the size of a layer cake that gives him headaches. She is in college in the city, and to his amazement, now that he is damaged, she's taken more of an interest in him, like the three-legged hamster she ministered to as a child. When Henry speaks to Margot, once a week by phone, she makes him feel as though his new life is a lunge from a moving vehicle. But Effie is Florence Nightingale to Henry's foot soldier, off in a war where the opposing armies touch penises. They're good together; raising her was the one thing he did well. She even wants to help him write a personal ad, for Craigslist or Manhunt or DaddyCentral or the cavalcade of humiliations online, but some things your daughter cannot help you do.

"CuriousFather," he types. It sounds strange to him, his new name, if it is a name. He decides he is Oral Versatile Bear, a box he'd never thought he'd have to check in this world. He crops Margot out of a vacation photograph and posts it.

Within an hour, he has responses. The first is from a teenager in Poughkeepsie who asks him if he has back hair. The second, from FurJock06, wants to know his feelings on

"cockfighting." He wades, blindly, through the acronyms—
NSA, PNP, 4:20, P.A., T but V—but the shorthand is endless.
A lanky, flawless young man named ThckReggie comes on
strong, asking him, "Wanna get off?" before he even knows
Henry's name. "Woof. You cam?" is Reggie's next message,
followed by a link to a pornographic website. When Henry
replies, Reggie seems not to listen or care. In fact, when
Reggie continues to message, Henry discovers Reggie is a
robot of some sort, and Henry finds another rung of indig-
nity. Self-esteem dissipating by the second, he e-mails the
kid in Poughkeepsie to report that he has back hair, yes. Two
wings across his shoulder blades that he never, in a million
years, would call an asset. The kid does not reply, will never
reply.

The next day, feeling frustrated and combustible, Henry
stops for gas and, across the cement island, a driver in sweat-
pants, sweatshirt, and sunglasses flashes him his penis, a
thumb in blackened grass. Henry looks around, unsure if he
is in the intended audience for a penis out in the daylight. But
yes, the view is his and his alone. It's all Henry needs to break
a sweat.

"You like?" the driver says, leaning against the flank of his
SUV.

"I do," Henry says. "I only saw it for a brief moment. But
it made an impression."

The driver nods. "I go for the coach type."

"You a big sports fan?" Henry asks, because it seems ger-
mane and is something he can say. But the other driver seems

not to hear him, or care, or has decided he is no longer the coach type. The gas pump clicks, he puts the nozzle back into the pump and settles back in his car.

"Wait, could I get your number?" Henry asks, but the other driver is already pulling out. Henry follows him, feeling confused and abbreviated. In a low-grade sex fever, he tracks the SUV into the wilds of Monmouth County. Finally, the other driver drives into the three-car garage of a suburban manse, and Henry parks at the curb, about to choke on the possibilities. Then the other driver steps out of his car—he's squatter, more thuggish than Henry remembers—and unmistakably shakes his head at Henry, decisively, brutally, *no*, and vanishes inside.

Henry decides that since he has come this far out of his way, he deserves something, the gift of a body at least. He crosses the front lawn and peeks in the bay window. Track lights halo a bowl of polished stones on a console table. Across the room, he can make out the colorful plastic of a child's play castle, and he's desperate enough to not to care if there's a baby in the vicinity. The baby can watch, honestly. Suddenly, he finds he is knocking at the front door, knowing with every step that he is moving somehow away from a person he understands.

A woman opens it, in a white blouse, working the earrings from her ear. "Can I help you?"

The other driver, Henry's prize, cowers on the stairs. Henry can feel his secret becoming a knife.

"I'm sorry," Henry says. "I must have the wrong address."

"Who are you looking for?" she asks, and Henry turns and runs.

Three weeks later, he's is on the train upstate to Dawn Manor. He's been instructed to get off at a small station where a van will pick him up. "We'll be doing bodywork," Bodi Charles told him over the phone. "Make sure to bring comfortable clothing." Henry gazes down his front. In the stress of the separation, with Effie's donuts and nachos for dinner, he no longer has comfortable clothing.

A nondescript minivan idles in the station lot. The driver, in a leather jacket and black T-shirt, jumps out and throws open the passenger door. He introduces himself as Spike, and his handshake, it reassures Henry to find, is vigorous with heterosexuality. Spike's face and scalp are as smooth as glazed ceramic except for a brown goatee so manicured it could be topiary. Henry finds he is the only passenger and sits as far back as possible.

The densely forested road gives way to acres of rolling hills. Henry feels out of joint in such an isolated and rustic place; if he's going to find himself, it's going to be somewhere off the Garden State Parkway, near Indian food and a Hobby Lobby. Spike turns into a long gravel driveway. A peace flag bolted to a roadside maple only increases Henry's sense of personal doom.

"Look, I've changed my mind. Could you take me back to the train station?"

Spike answers, "There's only one train a day."

"I'll stay at a hotel."

"There's no hotel."

"Then I'll call a cab," Henry says.

But Spike has already parked in front of the Manor, a three-story Victorian painted, of all possible colors, purple. A wooden double door, impeccably restored, opens onto a broad porch with a row of wooden rocking chairs. The house is surrounded by trees, as though they carved the property out of forest.

"You've come this far," Spike says. "Try going a little bit further."

Henry steps out of the van and closes his eyes. He takes a moment to notice the cold, a private sign that he is one year older. Soon, his December birthday will come and go and he may never answer the questions his body is asking.

Spike lifts his bag. "Also, you don't want to deal with the cancellation policy."

In the hardwood foyer, a pussy-willow branch teeters in a vase like an accusatory finger. Above the telephone stand hangs a photographic portrait of Rigby the retriever slavering in a swatch of autumn light. Henry counts six armchairs in the living room and nothing else. The place seems willfully under-decorated, as if everything might need to be rearranged or cleared for yoga or trust falls. This is precisely how Margot always wanted their home to be—airy, uncluttered. Perhaps now it is, since he was the clutter.

Spike leads Henry up the narrow stairs. "So no cell phone use inside the house, please. And no alcohol, no drugs, no sex, and no plastics. Bodi is environmentally sensitive."

"Plastics?" Henry asks.

"Some guys think they can bring their rubber gear any-where." Spike stops on the landing. "You have no idea what I'm talking about, do you?"

Henry's room is on the second floor, wedged under one of the gables. It's the sort of space people turn into a crypt of winter clothes and exercise equipment. A blond young man, Henry guesses midtwenties, lays on one of two twin beds like a deposited doll. He's dressed in a puffy orange hunting jacket and loafers without socks. With a small terror, Henry under-stands that this is his roommate.

"Jed," Spike says, "you know you can take off your jacket."

"Are there *no* single rooms?" Henry asks as kindly, diplo-matically, as possible. Jed snorts.

"Everybody gets a roommate," Spike explains, one hand on the doorknob, which, Henry notices, does not have a lock. "If we put people in singles, they just close off to the process."

"The process . . . ?" Henry says.

"Of integrating . . . And actualizing . . . Oh, don't ask me," Spike says. "I just cook and fluff the pussy willow." Spike leaves them to get acquainted, his boots—made for heavy construction—clomping down the stairs.

Jed eyes him bluntly with his sharp, blue eyes. "So are you gay?"

Henry sits on other bed. "I was married for twenty-two years . . ." he says, and then stops. He's not sure where the story goes after that.

Jed leans back. "Thank God."

———————

Dawn Manor's resident guru sits in a leather armchair in the living room, wearing a linen shirt and flowy pants that are basically drapes.

"It's the secrets that kill us," Bodi says. "And the cure for secrets is stories."

He's greyhound-thin, with rimless glasses and the flexibilities of a man half his age; every now and again, he lifts himself up on the armrests, like a gymnast on the bars, to tuck his feet and sit cross-legged. Henry has noticed how Bodi touches things—tabletops, shoulders—with intense, appraising grace. Bodi was an antiques dealer in "a prior life," he told them over breakfast. "It made me understand that everything has a delicacy that must be protected."

Four men face Bodi in a scattershot arrangement. Across from Henry, Jed sits on his hands and contemplates his kneecaps. Of the group, Henry is by far the oldest.

"How about you, Doug?" Bodi says, his hands resting upwards on his knees. "Tell us the story of your secret."

Doug's gaze relocates from the window to Bodi. He spooks Henry—in a cowboy shirt and stained jeans, Doug gives off stray voltage, mumbling his reluctance under his breath. Even his moustache doesn't look completely enlisted. Doug works a cigarette from his pocket and Bodi stops him.

"No smoking inside."

"I just want to roll it between my fingers," Doug says. "It helps me relax."

Doug explains that he worked in a shipyard in Bayonne, running the cranes, and "pruning up" in the showers. "I was Jiffy Lube. In and out," Doug says, and Henry shivers with a revulsion that almost instantly becomes intrigue. Doug's boss showed up in the showers, fucked him, and fired him the next day. "Those were *union* showers," Doug says. "Asshole was management."

He lights the cigarette and Bodi says, in a first show of authority, "Put the cigarette out or go outside." Doug smirks and heads out to the porch.

Bodi threshes his hands, recovering the moment. "Henry, what about you? Would you like to say something?"

Henry looks for an entrance, a beginning to what seems like hopeless years of middle. He sees the ghostly bridge of a forearm reaching into his sleeping bag at Boy Scout camp circa 1963. He remembers, as a teenager, imagining his parents dying in a plane crash so he could live with the tenor Jussi Björling in his Italian castle and hold his penis in his hand whenever he wanted to, the secret root of his talent. Then, with a stab of self-loathing, Henry recalls the certain fold and tuck to the coverlet on the guest bed, the way he remade it every time he raided his cache. "In the early part of my marriage," Henry starts, and it's like working a stone free from inside him. "I started this extension to my house that I never finished . . ."

At the edge of the driveway, Henry and three others stand in a confused huddle, trying to fix a snow break. Bodi sent them out to the lawn to work. "Across cultures, across time, men go outside to go inside," he told them. A day in, and the platitude per minute of speech ratio is getting to Henry. It's as if Bodi has learned to turn every sentence inside out, like a sock.

Henry holds a notched wooded brace while Doug sets two four-by-fours into it. Another man, short and talkative, hammers at the juncture point, missing the nail as much as not. His name tag, stuck to the outside of his jacket, reads "Ronnie!" He works as an inspector for the Transit Authority, which, he said earlier, means he can cruise every truck stop on the Turnpike while getting paid.

"I thought this was supposed to be some singles thing," Doug announces, blowing air into his fist. "Except it turns out I paid eight hundred bucks to fix this guy's fucking lawn."

Standing off to the side, Jed giggles in his jacket and loafers.

Doug shoots back, "You think eight hundred bucks is funny?"

Jed retracts his hands inside his sleeves and holes up.

Since the morning, Henry has been feeling increasingly distant, like he has tickets to his life except they're last row, obscured view. What did he come for? None of the men seem like prospects to him; they're all as warped and lonely as he is. With a pang, he realizes he's missing Van, back home, tending to his plants and mail. He must call.

Suddenly, a brown-black flutter of wings explodes from behind the trees. Canada geese, gathering into a migration.

Jed watches them, his mouth open. "How far do they go?"

"Delaware, Maryland, I think," Henry says.

"Outside Bethesda, some guy held a knife to my throat until I swallowed," Ronnie says. "That's Maryland in a nutshell."

Gunshots pop from behind the Manor, out of view. Henry flinches. Hunters. The geese go wild, squawking. "Shit, it's Vietnam up here," Doug says.

Then Henry notices that there are tears rolling down Jed's cheeks, and the kid makes no effort to wipe them away. "Are you all right?" he asks.

"It's something that happens sometimes, from my meds," Jed says. "I don't have control over it."

A bell peels at the front porch: Bodi calling them inside. Doug collects the tools and shoves them at Jed, saying, "You carry them, since you didn't do jack shit." The others head back, but Henry lingers with Jed. They're roommates, after all, and this is what roommates do. He notices, at his ankle, a little strip of skin. Even in the cold, the kid's not wearing any socks. Up close, out here in the bracing cold, he sees that Jed is older than he thought, with difficult skin. He's not so much young as preserved. Last night, in bed, Jed told him his father runs a Christian school in Pennsylvania. "Goliath was *uncircumcised*,'" Jed whispered. "That's what the Bible says." Henry turned off the light and said, "Look, don't give me nightmares."

Out in the dusk, Henry puts his hand on Jed's shoulder. With an expectant look, Jed follows Henry's hand to his face, registering a proposition.

"Am I attractive?" Jed asks.

Henry removes his hand. "Listen, kid, I'm not looking."

Jed's face goes flat. "You're too old anyway."

It's such a senselessly cruel thing to say. Henry leaves him, burdened with the tools, thinking, Go ahead and freeze.

Lunch is Spike in a T-shirt and cargo shorts, delivering their pork chops to the table and flexing his biceps. He could be working the leisure deck of a cruise.

"Should we save some food for Rigby?" Ronnie asks.

The question creates a strange quiet. Bodi straightens and Spike goes to him. Seeing them together, for the first time, Henry realizes this is partly what Dawn Manor sells, the miracle they're there for: two grown men, leaning into each other.

"Rigby passed away," Bodi says. "She had a stroke two weeks ago."

"It was horrible and spasmy," says Spike. "Like, *froth* was coming out of her mouth—"

"Please, Spike . . ." Bodi says. "We'll see you boys in an hour."

Spike and Bodi excuse themselves through a door marked "PRIVATE," their area of the house. A lock slides home.

"Guys," Ronnie says, "who do you think is cuter? Bodi or Spike?"

Doug crashes his fork to his plate. "We just heard about a fucking dog dying."

Henry decides he has to leave, before he turns into one of these people. He heads to the porch and finds a corner where his cell gets a single dot of service.

"Is there a sling?" Van asks when he answers.

"No."

"Oh, I thought for sure there'd be a sling."

"Jesus," Henry says. "Listen, I need to get out of here."

"Is it a cult?" Van says. "Tell me and I'll get the Better Business Bureau to do an airlift."

Henry hears, faintly, the clink of ice in a glass. "Are you drinking?" From the quiet he knows that he's right. But he's in no position to challenge anyone on their contradictions.

"Mmmm," Van says. "Survey says yes."

"Weren't you supposed to have your son this weekend?"

Van says his ex-wife just informed him she's moving to Orlando, and that she's taking his son with her. "Now I realize why people kidnap their children," Van says. "What's the jail time on that?"

"We have to look out for each other," Henry says. "You're my closest friend." He winces at the truth of it.

"I know," Van says, "and I just really feel bad about that."

Through the living room windows, Henry watches snow streak down, blanketing the lawn. A blizzard is beginning, and for two more days, he's going to be stuck here with these men trying to pry him open. Bodi hands out dozens of red strips of ribbon. They're supposed to tie one to each part of their bodies that has experienced a "wounding." "I did this at a men's conference in Sedona," Bodi says, "and by the end, there was just this *sea* of red."

Doug throws his ribbons to the floor.

"Nobody said this would be easy," Bodi says.

"Nobody said this bullshit works," Doug says. "I'm going out."

But with the front door wide, Doug stops short at the threshold. "Holy fuck," Doug says. "You might want to look at this."

Emblazoned across the door, in red spray paint, are letters. It takes Henry a moment to decode them, and then more time to understand that the graffiti refers to them. "FAGGOTS." He has never been called a faggot before, and now, in shock, he realizes he is hated for a love that he's yet to experience. Bodi rushes out to the porch and whispers, "Who the hell . . ." The whole front of the house is covered in it, a single brutal streak. Some neighbor kid practicing to use fear, Henry thinks. There's a call to the police and a terse negotiation about an incident report.

"How long until they get here?" Ronnie asks.

"Not long," Bodi says.

"Don't you pay taxes?" Ronnie says. He's clearly terrified. "There should be fences! Fences and guns!"

"You're overreacting," Bodi says.

"Of course I am," Ronnie says back. "It's what I'm good at!"

Henry notices Doug has vanished outside, to the lawn. "Should I get him?" During moments of stress, Henry wants assignments, distracting lists. It's the stage manager in him. Before he's out the door, Ronnie hands him a can of mace and whispers, "Remember Bethesda."

Out on the lawn, the snow slants horizontally in the wind. Henry spies Doug a ways up the drive, hammering at the snow break. Henry approaches with his hands in his pockets, like a sullen teen, but he feels a passing moment of luck, as though he has stepped out from underneath a bull's-eye. He wonders how Bodi will rescue the weekend. At least, Henry thrills to think, they'll skip the bodywork.

A bright orange flash moves at his periphery and Henry takes an instinctive step back. At the edge of the forest, a hunter emerges from the trees, dressed in camouflage uniform and cap. He carries a goose over his shoulder, its neck twisted like a gunnysack. In his left hand, a double-barrel shotgun points into the ground. The hunter nods to Henry as he turns to a pine tree and unzips his fly.

"You one of the gays?" the hunter calls out, pissing against the tree.

"Yes . . . ?" Henry says, and the hunter nods. "You didn't happen to see anyone around this property did you? There's graffiti all over the house. Just happened."

The hunter looks back, not bothering to conceal himself on the turn. "Somebody did a little job, eh?" he says, and shakes off, tucking himself back in. "No idea, but I'll tell you this. You know that dog they had running around here? Getting into people's business?"

"Actually, I don't. I just got here."

"Well, you tell the boys who live here I know who poisoned her."

"Why are you telling me this?"

The hunter spits something dark and infernal into the snow. "Because everybody's had a dog. Even if it wasn't a dog."

Some bullshit rural koan Henry won't bother to unravel. He only wanted to slip in and out of this place a better, less-confused person. He never wanted to be a messenger, an actor in anything. The weekend pivots into greater darkness.

"Evening," the hunter says, and heads back into the trees.

Henry rushes back to the Manor, determined to throw this information off him, rid his mind of it. The dead animal, the graffiti, these aren't his problems. He has his own pile.

When he reenters the living room, Spike has made a fire.

"I need to talk to you," Henry says. "I just met one of your neighbors."

Bodi makes him tell the story twice. Ronnie gasps at every detail until Bodi shoots him a chilling look. A hard rap hits the front door, and the men go silent. Henry's pulse skips, imagining a mob outside with torches, pitchforks, hoes—rusty, upstate kind of weapons.

"Don't open the door!" Ronnie yells, and moves behind one of the armchairs. "It's a trap! I saw this movie!"

"Who is it?" Bodi asks.

"Is this Dawn Manor?" a familiar voice asks. Bodi unlatches the door and the radiator in Henry's chest takes a kick, fires on. Van walks into the parlor in his corduroy jacket, hiking boots, a long knit cap folded in his hands like an offering.

"Hey," Van says. "Did I miss the fun part?"

Spike recognizes the hunter by the detail of the beard, a man named Bailey, and calls. Bailey informs him that one of their neighbors, a widow, paid two high school kids to feed Rigby a steak laced with ketamine. Retribution, Henry learns, for some damage the dog caused to a pheasant farm.

"I've done ketamine," Spike tells Bodi. "And I can tell you it is so deeply fucked up that I can't even tell you."

Henry stands with them, corralled as the witness, watching Van mix with the crowd in the living room. The fact that his friend, his possession, is socializing with others bothers him immeasurably. "Can I go?" he asks, and it triggers Spike's sense of action.

"We need to talk to this woman tonight."

"That's absurd," Bodi says.

And Spike answers, eyebrows raised, "Really? You want to tell me about absurd?" and Henry glimpses into their private dynamic, the corners of dismissal and condescension. As he edges away, leaving them to argue, the last thing he hears is Spike saying, with vivifying power, "If we bring the police into this, we look like cowards, and this gay man is *not* a coward," and Bodi replying, "Would you stop saying '*this gay man*,' please?"

In the parlor, Van sits on the floor, rubbing his eyes. His shirtsleeves are rolled back and, in the firelight, his forearms look lathed, crafted, tended to. Van pats the back of Henry's calf, a contact that blooms.

"So are you Henry's boyfriend?" Ronnie asks.

"I'm more of an evacuation team," Van answers. A flask sheathed in leather nestles between his legs. "Is somebody going to explain the writing on the outside of this place?"

"Drinking's not allowed," Henry says.

"Yeah, well," Doug says, nabbing the flask, "this whole weekend is off the handle." He drinks and dashes it back to Van when Bodi approaches.

With a tight, dark expression—a coerced look Henry recognizes from his own marriage—Bodi explains that they're going out, to meet this woman and try to resolve things. Ronnie tells him that they're crazy to leave, but Spike will not be delayed.

"The roads are nutsy," Van says. "But do what you gotta do."

Bodi turns to Henry. "I'm asking you to be in charge while we're gone. And please everyone stay inside." Another job Henry didn't ask for, does not want. The two men gather their jackets and are gone. Left to themselves, the men look at each other tentatively, as though some central part of the architecture—the force holding them, and the entire situation, together—had just been removed.

"Can we talk for a minute?" Henry says to Van. "In my room."

"*Our* room," Jed says.

On the stairs, Van slinks behind him, which makes Henry feel like a scold. Once in the garret, Van stretches out on the bed, his eyes red and raw. "You wouldn't believe the roads," he says. "Remember that production of *A Christmas Carol* where the snow-rigging broke? And like mounds of it ended up on the stage?" He pulls his legs to his chest, one at a time, to stretch them, as though he'd come from some exertion.

"Are you high?" Henry asks.

Van stops and considers the ceiling. "God, Mrs. Cratchit had great tits."

"Drunk *and* high?"

Van sits up on the edge of the bed and nods solemnly. "I know, I'm a disaster."

Henry sits across from him. Van is living in the same pair of corduroys, same plaid shirt he last saw him in.

"Why did you come?" Henry asks, hoping for one kind of answer.

"I was going out of my mind in my place," Van says. "You gave me a mission."

Van rises and casually sifts through the closet. Out comes a stack of handkerchiefs in different colors. "Is there some kind of karate belt system for gay dudes that I'm not aware of?"

"They're my roommate's," Henry says, finding relief in a subject that is not either of them. "Jed."

"Which one's Jed?"

"The drugged-up little monster. I'm sure you saw him."

Van pulls a brown pill bottle from the closet and examines the label. With a whistle, he says, "Haldol. This is the serious shit."

At that, Henry sees the door crack open and Jed lets himself in, without knocking. Van tries to shove the pills back into the closet.

"What are you doing?" Jed asks.

"I'm looking for . . ." Van says, "this." It is an iron.

Jed goes to his mattress and stares at them both emptily. "It's late. What are you trying to iron?"

Van tests its weight in his hand. "Just wanted to know if there was one. Make and model."

Van is not a good liar when he's sober, but intoxicated, he's pathetic. Jed goes to the closet and studies his shelf for damage. "You weren't looking for that. You were going through my things."

"Oh, come on, Jed," Henry says. "He's just goofing around."

"You just called me a drugged-up monster. I heard you."

Henry sighs. He and Jed, the oldest and the youngest, are the two last boys to be picked for the team, and they need to band together. "We're all trying here," Henry says, but trying for what? To be themselves, finally, and it is goddamn exhausting.

"I'm going to take a walk," Jed says.

It's plainly a bad idea, but Henry wants his time with Van, and he won't stop him.

"Knock yourself out," Van says.

Once Jed is gone—they listen for his footsteps on the stairs—Henry whispers, "You see what this place is like."

Van lies on the bed, against Henry, oblivious to his power. "Maybe it's good for you," he says. "We both know you need to get over me." And the shock of its delivery detonates. All these months, Van knew his secret desire and now speaks it aloud like a boring headline.

Henry wills himself to grab for what he loves. He rests his

hand on Van's knee, the closest he can come. "I don't think that's true."

Van pats Henry's hand. "I'm on the wrong team, buddy."

Henry feels the moment between them dilating, narrowing to a point. "I don't think you're on anybody's team."

Van lifts Henry's hand off his thigh and deposits it on the mattress. "And now I will avail myself of a libation," he says, and heads out. Henry hammers his pillow. The question that he came up here to answer—who can I love?—is not a question after all. It is an impossibility. The downstairs phone rings and continues to ring. Henry yells for someone to answer it. Finally, the ringing stops, and in the silence, he hears music.

Downstairs, the men are missing, but the door into Spike and Bodi's private area is open. From inside comes the murmur of voices and a heavy muddle of incense. He enters, through a long hallway, which opens to a living room where Van and the others have collected, sipping from coffee cups. The room is cramped, more like a passageway converted into a parlor, with Van smoking a joint in an overbuilt recliner in the center of the room, like a cockpit for television consumption. Ronnie attends to the stereo, setting a Judy Collins song on the turntable, while Doug, sways back and forth on a loveseat, mouthing the lyrics.

"Welcome, Chief," Van says coolly, and offers him a toke. Henry grits his teeth and tries to stare accountability into him.

"This is a really bad idea," Henry says.

Ronnie combs through the LPs. "This really might be the gayest record collection on the planet."

"Is there any Cher?" Doug says with his eyes closed. "Please let there be Cher."

As a stage manager, Henry is known for his quiet control and firm hand, but now he sees the fantasy of it. He has no intrinsic authority, only what is given to him. So he takes a seat on the couch next to Doug and surrenders. When Doug passes the joint, Henry takes a single, ferocious inhale, welcoming the chance for a new personality.

"So Van, if you're not Henry's boyfriend," Ronnie asks, "are you anybody's boyfriend?"

Van grins and there's this one crazy tooth that can still break Henry's loyal heart. It's as if he wants to pass here, among them. Ronnie swings around to Van's side and gives Van a shoulder massage with a boldness Henry can only imagine. "You know you have great hair," Ronnie says. "It's muy *Pirates of Penzance*." The recliner shifts back another notch, setting Van more prone.

"I took a Body Electric class once," Ronnie says.

"Is that where they call it massage but you just end up jerking each other off?" Doug asks. It is, based on the longing in his face, a genuine question. Henry's thoughts drift toward a class that is also, somehow, quasi-public group sex, and how anything gets done.

Ronnie dismisses Doug. "People think that because people are ashamed of their own body's capacity for pleasure."

"So it is about jerking each other off."

"Jesus," Ronnie says.

"Whatever you're doing feels awesome," Van says and begins, with drunken volition, a story about his ten-year-old son, his soccer games, and his growing pains, "leg cramps that got so bad he'd just ball up and cry."

"You're a dad?" Ronnie says.

Van marvels at a private happiness. "Yeah. You should try it. It's amazing."

Ronnie asks, "Where's he now?"

Van doesn't answer, seems to fall into himself. Ronnie's hands pinch and knead his shoulders in what is a definitively nonerotic, fully half-assed massage. Ronnie mouths to Henry, *Oh my God, did he die?*

Henry sits up, summoned back into the present moment. "Look, just leave him alone."

"What'd I do?" Ronnie says.

"Can't you see he's upset?"

But when Ronnie retracts his hand, Van grabs it and keeps it on him. He swipes his face and replies, "It's fine. Keep going."

Ronnie goes back to the massage and Van groans, a sound in their years of friendship Henry has never heard him make. With that single sound, the room suddenly seems more dense, a hot close dream. A tiny metallic clack: Doug undoing his belt. "That's right," Doug says, his eyes jumping all over Van's body, like he's checking to see how pieces of machinery come together. He kneels at Van's side and rubs the inseam of Van's pants and Van flinches.

"Just relax," Doug says.

"What are you doing?" Henry asks quietly.

Doug pulls Van's shirt up out of his waist and Henry catches a glimpse of a white blade of flesh at Van's groin before he closes his eyes.

He hears the rustle and give of the leather recliner, the rake of Ronnie's fingers. The teeth of a zipper giving way. It would be so easy for Henry to join. He's close enough to feel the transgression with his hands. "Fuck yeah," Doug says over and over, in a hungry loop.

He can't watch Van be taken, fed upon. There are certain rules to things. Aren't there rules? Henry walks calmly, decisively, out of the room, taking the stairs two a time, back to his room, where he sits on the bed, disoriented, his blood thumping. He throws open the window and gulps in the cold. Across the lawn, Jed, in his orange coat, treks in the fresh snow at the perimeter of the house lights. Henry calls out to him, the other exile, but Henry discovers he has nothing to say. So he waves hello. Jed waves back, sweetly, like they're two boys departing from each other after an evening of play. Then he moves further and further out until Henry can no longer see him at all.

Henry wakes up in his clothes. He stares at Jed's bed across the room until he realizes that it is immaculate, the way Jed had left it the night before. He never came back from his walk. The morning assembles itself, finally, as an emergency.

He searches the other rooms, the bathroom. Nothing. He's

not inside. Downstairs, Henry finds Van on the living room floor, cocooned in a crocheted blanket. His shoes and socks are off and Henry sees on Van's foot a little meadow of hair split by a scar, a scar about which Henry will never know the story.

Henry nudges him awake. "What?" Van asks, bleary, and Henry stares at his face, slack from sleep, the closest he'll ever come. And he feels nothing, the end of an idea. It's not a kiss Henry wants, but a chance to be known, fully, in this life.

Henry says, "You need to leave."

"Now?" Van says.

"Now."

Bodi enters the living room and gives Henry a noncommittal nod. He's not angry, or at least he's oblivious; the men must have cleaned up, erased the night from the room. They will get away with it. Nothing will be noticed. Bodi goes to the front window to stare at the feet of snow piled on the lawn, the heap of the night's weather.

"Everything went all right last night?" Bodi asks.

"Jed's missing," Henry says. "He went for a walk and never came back."

Bodi's face falls. "Oh, Christ, my fucking insurance."

He rings the house bell and Doug and Ronnie collect in the foyer, purposefully missing each other's eyes. "The kid went AWOL?" Doug asks. "Could have called that."

Bodi asks them to go looking, and Henry's first to be outside, happy to be free of the house. He punches through the snow, going to the trees, where he last saw Jed. At the edge of the forest, he turns back to look at the other men, splintering across the lawn. Van's at his car, wiping the snow from the windshield, preparing to go. They see each other, for a moment, a final view, until Henry turns away. By Monday, Van will have quit and be moving to Florida.

About fifty yards into the trees, Henry comes across Jed's body, propped against a spruce. At some point in the night, Jed unbuttoned his orange jacket, with nothing underneath. No shirt, just his skin exposed to the air and covered by a light ramp of snow. Henry kneels beside him, and Jed's eyes open and find him. His face is glazed, but he's alive. Inside the lining of Jed's jacket, tucked in the pocket, is the spray paint can with a red cap.

"Leave me here," Jed says, barely over a whisper. "I'm not right."

Henry takes the cylinder of paint from the jacket and palms it. The metal is frigid to the touch, nearly empty, and the ball clacks inside. Henry tosses the can into the woods, as far as he can. It's a good throw, a good release. "You're coming with me," Henry says, committing to it. Then he curls his arms around the boy and lifts.

ACKNOWLEDGMENTS

Deepest thanks to the editors who helped me with these stories: Hannah Tinti, Michael Ray, Andrew Snee, C. Michael Curtis. To the persevering Nathaniel Jacks at InkWell and the wonderful Emily Cunningham at HarperCollins, who believed. To the teachers along the way, Don Faulkner, Jackson Taylor, Sam Lipsyte, Samantha Chang, Jill McCorkle, Margot Livesey, Adam Haslett, and others. To friends and readers for encouragement and bullshit meters: Caitlin Horrocks, John Krokidas, Brian Leung, Josh Spanogle, Yahlin Chang, Kevin Moffett, Matthew Vollmer, Corinna Vallianatos, Mara Naselli, Nina Siegel, Nic Brown, Leslie Jamison, Anna Solomon, Michael Balliro. To my family, Colin, Mary, April, Mom, Slinky, and Bob.

About the Author

Read on

Insights,
Interviews
& More . . .

Meet Austin Bunn

AUSTIN BUNN is a fiction writer, playwright, screenwriter, and former journalist. His writing has appeared in *The Atlantic Monthly, Zoetrope, The New York Times Magazine, Wired, Best American Science and Nature Writing, The Pushcart Prize*, and elsewhere. He cowrote the screenplay to *Kill Your Darlings* (Sony Pictures Classics), starring Daniel Radcliffe, Dane DeHaan, and Michael C. Hall, which premiered at the Sundance Film Festival. He is a graduate of Yale University and the University of Iowa Writers' Workshop, and a recipient of a Michener-Copernicus Fellowship. Currently, he teaches at Cornell University in Ithaca, New York. ◠

A Conversation with Austin Bunn

A dialogue with Austin Bunn about
The Brink *and his writing process.*
Questions were posed by his editor
at Harper Perennial.

How did you latch on to the idea of
"the brink" as one that would guide
your work?

Like millions of us growing up in the
late 1980s, I grew up terrified of nuclear
war. Nevil Shute's riveting novel *On the*
Beach—about survivors of WWIII living
out their last days in Australia—was
bedtime reading. In the era of mutually
assured destruction, I was convinced I'd
never make it to adulthood. Eventually,
I got distracted by Robert Cormier
novels, dream research (aka watching
my best friend sleep and taking notes),
and filming new scenes for a horror
film called *Grondak IV* on VHS.
My insecurities became more social,
suburban. By the time I was an awkward,
sarcastic, undeniably annoying teenager
with an Ogilvy Home Perm (maybe—
probably—yep, gay), I was discovering
there was life on the other side of my
anxiety—the annihilation of one version
of yourself didn't mean that you were
over. That link has drawn me to stories
about the resilience and transformations
that happen at that moment when one
way of life ends and another begins.
I was always somehow jealous of the
fiction writers who seemed capable of ▶

3

deciding on a theme or topic and
exploring it prismatically (as in Adam
Haslett's *You Are Not a Stranger Here*, or
Jennifer Egan's *A Visit from the Goon
Squad*—both tremendous models). But
my imagination just wouldn't organize
itself that way. So while I never set
out to write stories about these "brinks,"
I just discovered, when I read them all
together, they circled around the same
theme. Our obsessions reveal us.

*What do you make of the apocalyptic
or post-apocalyptic trend that has
taken fiction, and particularly young
adult fiction, by storm? How do you
think this collection fits into that
trend?*

I spent seventh and eighth grade
writing apocalyptic short stories—the
apocalypse was the only thing I really
felt comfortable writing about. And
as far as I could tell, the apocalyptic
sublime had long been literary gold:
Poe's *The Narrative of Arthur Gordon Pym*,
Shackleton's Antarctic misadventures,
Stephen King's *The Stand* and the
Bachman Books, Lovecraft's "At the
Mountains of Madness," Camus's *The
Plague*, Thomas Disch's *The Genocides*,
Harlan Ellison's "I Have No Mouth
and I Must Scream." . . . One thing
fiction is good for is giving your mind's
eye something truly terrifying to think
about: making your way through a
dark Holland Tunnel full of corpses;
life inside a machine that has taken

over the planet; or an endless walk
that is both a game and death march.

It's the notion of a teenaged (and often
female) protagonist in these newest
scenarios—in a world of unparented
other teens—that strikes me as genuinely
novel and honors the anxieties of the
echo-boom population of new readers.
What I appreciate the most is their
metabolism: the trust in pure story and
propulsion. I like to think the stories in
The Brink share some of the unnerving
appeal of an off-kilter world and the raw
nerve of change.

**What is your draft process? Where do
these stories begin?**

When I begin drafting, I start with
voice—the dramatist in me *hears* a story
first: I think about register, attack,
urgency. Chuck Palahniuk (and he would
credit his mentor Tom Spanbauer for
this) talks about "burnt tongue"—the
idea that your protagonist enters the
fiction needing to talk, having just
survived something. For me, the first-
person story was my starting point. The
testimonial tradition (in stories like
"Ledge" and "The End of the Age Is
Upon Us") has a relationship to the
monologue in ways that I'm still
understanding and exploring. Both my
parents were language teachers, and it's
voice that grabs me first. That said, I'm a
traditionalist when it comes to story
structure. I believe fiction's job is to show
us some kind of encounter with ▶

difficulty and ultimately a choice, a sense of agency. It might be a limitation of mine, but I want to think stories do something for us, that we read for a reason, which is to understand transition. The short story is the ideal form for a distillation of those elements. So I hammer and hammer on story, trying to grasp where the narrative wants to go. And once I find an ending, then I spend days making the trip as vivid as I can.

One of the big questions about story collections for authors is know when they are done. What made you decide the book was finished?

Honestly? Failure. I had a novella I'd been working on for months that became years that became a file-cabinet drawer's worth of notes, drafts, excisions, drawings (seriously), carefully curated encouraging feedback from friends that I consulted during my creative melancholias. . . . Screenwriters talk about "breaking a story," and I like the resonance of that, that the narrative is wild and uncontrollable, and you need to rein it in. This one story just wouldn't break. I had long imagined this novella as the capstone piece to the collection, but when I found myself revising its first page for the nth time, I finally decided to abandon it and see if the book could stand without it. Now I don't even miss it. Letting it go was the most freeing thing I've ever done. I highly recommend it.

You're a playwright, screenwriter, and fiction writer and have worked as a journalist. How do all these genres influence your fiction?

I've always been promiscuous genre-wise, and I can't help but think that's that part of the zeitgeist: novelist David Benioff writing for television, journalists like Mark Boal moving into film, filmmakers writing books. . . . It's all writing. I always admired the writers with range—Joan Didion, John Sayles, Jess Walter, all of whom write nonfiction, novels, films. My own creative instincts tend to go to scene writing, even as a journalist, and in that way, they spill in a variety of directions. Increasingly, I've come to find the consolations of prose—the things that books do that other forms such as film don't, like consciousness and interiority—a deep artistic reward. But one thing screenwriting teaches is economy, and how to have indefatigable energy and openness when it comes to revising. You have to keep showing up. You just have to. Then, one day, you look up and you're done. ᖫ

Austin Bunn Recommends

AMONG DOZENS of astoundingly good writers I might recommend— Kevin Brockmeier, Annie Dillard, Jess Walter, Sam Lipsyte, David Mitchell— I include these as potentially unexpected inspirations for the book in your hand.

Blindness, José Saramago: An absolutely mesmerizing speculative fiction about an epidemic of blindness that overtakes a South American city.

Selected Stories, Philip K. Dick: The metaphysical dilemmas, wrapped up in utterly accessible and driving science fiction.

War Fever, J. G. Ballard: What I love most about Ballard's heady, sinister stories is their formal restlessness. In one story, a series of reports from within an unmanned space station turns into a Borgesian exploration of infinite scale. In another, the answers to a questionnaire reveal an assassination plot that boggles the mind.

Close Range, Annie Proulx: For muscle tone.

Childhood's End, Arthur C. Clarke: The kind of book you read one way as a teenager and another way as an adult. It's wickedly difficult to craft such tectonic shifts in perception, but this book has one for the ages. ❧